ROYAL COURT

The Royal Court Theatre presents

THE PASS

by **John Donnelly**

The Pass was first performed at the Royal Court Jerwood Theatre Upstairs, Sloane Square, on Monday 13th January 2014.

THE PASS

by **John Donnelly**

Cast in order of appearance
Jason **Russell Tovey**
Ade **Gary Carr**
Lyndsey **Lisa McGrillis**
Harry **Nico Mirallegro**

Director **John Tiffany**
Designer **Laura Hopkins**
Lighting Designer **Chahine Yavroyan**
Sound Designer **Carolyn Downing**
Movement Director **Eddie Kay**
Stage Managers **Sarah Hellicar & Sophie Rubenstein**
Stage Management Work Placement **Fiona Davis**
Assistant Director **Holly Race Roughan**
Production Manager **Niall Black**
Costume Supervisor **Jackie Orton**

The Royal Court and Stage Management wish to thank the following for their help with this production:
Tim@kitking.co.uk, Ridiculous Solutions, Vicki Manderson, Morven Christie

THE COMPANY

JOHN DONNELLY (Writer)

FOR THE ROYAL COURT: Bone.

OTHER THEATRE INCLUDES: The Seagull (Headlong); Little Russians (Tricycle); The Knowledge (Bush); Encourage the Others (Almeida Projects); Songs of Grace & Redemption (Liminal); Burning Bush (Synergy/Unicorn); Conversation #1 (The Factory).

TELEVISION INCLUDES: Henry.

AWARDS INCLUDE: The Tom Erhardt Award, the PMA Award & the NSDF Sunday Times Playwriting Award.

GARY CARR (Ade)

THEATRE INCLUDES: Earthquakes in London, Nation, Dido Queen of Carthage (National); Marianne (Trafalgar Studios).

TELEVISION INCLUDES: Downton Abbey, Death in Paradise, Bluestone 42, George Gently, Silent Witness, Death in Paradise, Frankenstein's Wedding, Hominid: Neanderthal, Foyle's War, Law & Order, Silent Witness, Holby City, Runaway.

CAROLYN DOWNING (Sound Designer)

FOR THE ROYAL COURT: Circle Mirror Transformation, The Low Road, The Witness, Our Private Life, Oxford Street, Alaska.

OTHER THEATRE INCLUDES: Chimerica, Blood Wedding (Almeida); Handbagged (Tricycle); Beautiful Burnout (Frantic Assembly/National Theatre of Scotland); Love Song, Little Dogs (Frantic Assembly); Protest Song, Double Feature (National); King John, The Gods Weep, The Winter's Tale, Pericles, Days of Significance (RSC); Lower Ninth, Dimetos, Absurdia (Donmar); All My Sons (Schoenfeld Theatre, New York); Fanny och Alexander (Malmö Stadsteater); Amerika, Krieg der Bilder (Staatstheater Mainz, Germany); Tre Kroner - Gustav III (Dramaten, Sweden); Angels in America (Headlong); Blackta, After Miss Julie (Young Vic); To Kill A Mockingbird, The Country Wife, A Whistle in the Dark, Moonshed (Royal Exchange, Manchester); Andersen's English, Flight Path (Out Of Joint); Gone To Earth (Shared Experience); The Water Engine (503/Young Vic); Stallerhof (Southwark Playhouse); Lulu, The Kreutzer Sonata, Vanya, State Of Emergency, The Internationalist (Gate).

OPERA INCLUDES: How The Whale Became (ROH, Linbury); American Lulu (The Opera Group); After Dido (ENO).

EXHIBITIONS INCLUDE: Collider (Science Museum).

LAURA HOPKINS (Designer)

THEATRE INCLUDES: The Seagull (Headlong); Troilus & Cressida (RSC/Wooster Group); Beautiful Burnout (UK tour); A Delicate Balance (Almeida); Too Clever by Half, You Can't Take it with You (Royal Exchange, Manchester); King Lear (National, Chile); Lullaby, Gross Indecency, The Class Club (Duckie); Black Watch, Peter Pan, The House of Bernarda Alba (National Theatre of Scotland); Kellerman, Hotel Methuselah (Imitating the Dog); Time & the Conways (National); Faustus (Royal & Derngate, Northampton/Headlong); Hamlet, Othello (Royal & Derngate, Northampton); The Merchant of Venice (RSC); Peer Gynt (Guthrie); Golden Ass, Macbeth, Storm (Globe); Mister Heracles, Jerusalem (West Yorkshire Playhouse).

OPERA INCLUDES: Cosi Fan Tutte (ENO); Falstaff (ENO/Opera North); Elixir of Love (New Zealand Opera); Swan Lake Re-mixed (Volksoper, Vienna); The Rake's Progress (Welsh National Opera).

INSTALLATION/OTHER INCLUDES: The INS Broadcasting Unit (ICA); The INS London Declaration on Inauthenticity (Tate Britain).

EDDIE KAY (Movement Director)

AS CHOREOGRAPHER & MOVEMENT DIRECTOR, THEATRE INCLUDES: The Blue Boy, Have I No Mouth (Brokentalkers); Smiler (National Theatre of Scotland), Crash Test Human (Freshness).

AS RESIDENT MOVEMENT DIRECTOR, THEATRE INCLUDES: Once.

DANCE INCLUDES: Cost of Living, To Be Straight With You (DV8); Hymns, Dirty Wonderland, Othello, Beautiful Burnout (Frantic Assembly); Knots, As You Are, Faun (CoisCéim); Bird with Boy, The Falling Song (Junk Ensemble); Track (Brokentalkers).

OPERA INCLUDES: Dr Dee (Rufus Norris & Damon Albarn).

FILM INCLUDES: Cost of Living, Round 10, Motion Sickness.

LISA MCGRILLIS (Lyndsey)

THEATRE INCLUDES: : The Pitmen Painters (National); The Awkward Squad (Arts); Much Ado About Nothing, The Globe Mysteries (Globe); The Pitmen Painters (Manhattan Theatre Club); Hansel & Gretel, Tattercoats (Northern Stage); A Sock in the Wash, Nicole, The Pitmen Painters (Live).

TELEVISION INCLUDES: George Gently, Hebburn, Rocket Man, Spit Game

FILM INCLUDES: Much Ado About Nothing, The Other Possibility,

NICO MIRALLEGRO (Harry)

Nico is making his professional stage debut in The Pass.

TELEVISION INCLUDES: The Village, My Mad Fat Diary, Upstairs Downstairs, The Body Farm, Exile, Moving On.

FILM INCLUDES: Spike Island, McQueen, Six Minutes of Freedom, Common, Anita B.

HOLLY RACE ROUGHAN (Assistant Director)

AS ASSISTANT DIRECTOR, THEATRE INCLUDES: Adult Supervision (Park); The Birthday Party, A Doll's House, Three Birds, Rat's Tales, The Country Wife (Royal Exchange, Manchester); A Streetcar Named Desire, Nine Short Films (Arts Ed).

AS A DIRECTOR, THEATRE INCLUDES: Pages From My Songbook (Royal Exchange, Manchester); Believers Anonymous (Rosemary Branch); My Heart Can Whisper (White Bear); Waiting For Alice (Pleasance Courtyard); After the War (Cambridge ADC); Playhouse Creatures (MR5C Studio); Don Juan in Soho (Alma Tavern).

Holly was Resident Assistant Director at the Royal Exchange, Manchester (2012-13).

JOHN TIFFANY (Director)

FOR THE ROYAL COURT: Let the Right One In, Death Tax (Open Court).

OTHER THEATRE INCLUDES: Macbeth, Enquirer (co-director), The Missing, Peter Pan, The House of Bernarda Alba, Transform Caithness: Hunter, Be Near Me, Nobody Will Ever Forgive Us, The Bacchae, Black Watch, Elizabeth Gordon Quinn, Home: Glasgow (National Theatre of Scotland); Once (West End/Broadway); The Glass Menagerie (Broadway/American Repertory); Jerusalem (West Yorkshire Playhouse); Las Chicas de Tres Y Media Floppies (Granero, Mexico City); If Destroyed True (& Dundee Rep); Mercury Fur, The Straits, Helmet (Paines Plough); Gagarin Way, Abandonment, Among Unbroken Hearts, Passing Places (Traverse).

AWARDS INCLUDE: Tony, Lortell & Drama Desk Awards (Once); Laurence Olivier Award for Best Director, Critics' Circle Award for Best Director, South Bank Show Award (all for Black Watch).

John is an Associate Director at the Royal Court. From 2010 to 2011, he was a Radcliffe Fellow at Harvard University.

RUSSELL TOVEY (Jason)

FOR THE ROYAL COURT: A Miracle, Plasticine.

OTHER THEATRE INCLUDES: Sex With A Stranger (Trafalgar Studios); The Sea (Theatre Royal Haymarket); A Respectable Wedding (Young Vic); Tintin (Barbican); The History Boys (&West End/ Broadway), His Dark Materials, His Girl Friday, Henry V, Howard Katz (National); The Recruiting Officer (Chichester Festival).

TELEVISION INCLUDES: Looking, Talking to the Dead, What Remains, The Job Lot, Walking the Dogs, New Cross, Sherlock, Him & Her, Being Human, The Increasingly Poor Decisions of Todd Margaret,

Little Dorrit, Ashes to Ashes, Doctor Who, Annually Retentive, Gavin & Stacey, My Family & Other Animals, Poirot: Evil Under the Sun.

FILM INCLUDES: Pride, The Muppets, Blackwood, Effie Gray, Tower Block, Grabbers, Roar, Drop, In Passing, Pirates, Huge, The History Boys, The Emperor's New Clothes.

AWARDS INCLUDE: RTS Award for Best Comedy Performance (Him & Her).

CHAHINE YAVROYAN (Lighting Designer)

FOR THE ROYAL COURT: Let the Right One In, Narrative, Get Santa, Wig Out!, Relocated, The Lying Kind, Almost Nothing, At the Table, Bazaar, Another Wasted Year.

OTHER THEATRE INCLUDES: King Lear, The House, Major Barbara (Abbey, Dublin); A Soldier in Every Son, Measure for Measure, Marat/Sade, Dunsinane (& National Theatre of Scotland), God in Ruins, Little Eagles (RSC); Farewell, Half a Glass of Water (Field Day); Uncle Vanya (Minerva); The Lady from the Sea, The Comedy of Errors, Three Sisters (Royal Exchange, Manchester); Scorched (Old Vic Tunnels); FuenteOvejuna, Punishment Without Revenge, Dr. Faustus (Madrid); Elizabeth Gordon Quinn, Caledonia, Realism, The Wonderful World of Dissocia (National Theatre of Scotland); Orphans, Dallas Sweetman, Long Time Dead (Paines Plough); Dr. Marigold & Mr Chops (Riverside Studios); Jane Eyre, Someone Who'll Watch Over Me (Perth); Il Tempo del Postino (Manchester International Festival); How to Live (Barbican), & countless People Shows.

DANCE INCLUDES: Jasmin Vardimon Dance, Bock & Vincenzi, Frauke Requardt, Colin Poole, CanDoCo, Ricochet, Rosemary Lee, Arthur Pita.

MUSIC WORK INCLUDES: XX Scharnhorst (HMS Belfast), Sevastopol, Home (ROH2); Plague Songs (Barbican); Dalston Songs (ROH2); The Death of Klinghoffer (Scottish Opera); Jocelyn Pook Ensemble, Diamanda Galas (International).

SITE SPECIFIC WORK INCLUDES: Focal Point (Rochester Harbour); Enchanted Parks (Newcastle); Dreams of a Winter Night (Belsay Hall); Deep End (Marshall St Baths); Ghost Sonata (Sefton Park, Palmhouse).

THE ENGLISH STAGE COMPANY
AT THE ROYAL COURT THEATRE

'For me the theatre is really a religion or way of life. You must decide what you feel the world is about and what you want to say about it, so that everything in the theatre you work in is saying the same thing ... A theatre must have a recognisable attitude. It will have one, whether you like it or not.'

photo: Stephen Cummiskey

George Devine, first artistic director of the English Stage Company: notes for an unwritten book.

As Britain's leading national company dedicated to new work, the Royal Court Theatre produces new plays of the highest quality, working with writers from all backgrounds, and addressing the problems and possibilities of our time.

"The Royal Court has been at the centre of British cultural life for the past 50 years, an engine room for new writing and constantly transforming the theatrical culture." Stephen Daldry

Since its foundation in 1956, the Royal Court has presented premieres by almost every leading contemporary British playwright, from John Osborne's Look Back in Anger to Caryl Churchill's A Number and Tom Stoppard's Rock 'n' Roll. Just some of the other writers to have chosen the Royal Court to premiere their work include Edward Albee, John Arden, Richard Bean, Samuel Beckett, Edward Bond, Leo Butler, Jez Butterworth, Martin Crimp, Ariel Dorfman, Stella Feehily, Christopher Hampton, David Hare, Eugène Ionesco, Ann Jellicoe, Terry Johnson, Sarah Kane, David Mamet, Martin McDonagh, Conor McPherson, Joe Penhall, Lucy Prebble, Mark Ravenhill, Simon Stephens, Wole Soyinka, Polly Stenham, David Storey, Debbie Tucker Green, Arnold Wesker and Roy Williams.

"It is risky to miss a production there." Financial Times

In addition to its full-scale productions, the Royal Court also facilitates international work at a grass-roots level, developing exchanges which bring young writers to Britain and sending British writers, actors and directors to work with artists around the world. The research and play development arm of the Royal Court Theatre, The Studio, finds the most exciting and diverse range of new voices in the UK. The Studio runs play-writing groups including the Young Writers Programme, Critical Mass for Black, Asian and minority ethnic writers and the biennial Young Writers Festival. For further information, go to www.royalcourttheatre.com/playwriting/the-studio.

Supported by
ARTS COUNCIL
ENGLAND

New Season
Jan–Aug 2014

Jerwood Theatre Downstairs

30 Jan – 22 Mar
The Mistress Contract
By Abi Morgan
Based on the true story of a
remarkably unconventional couple.

3 Apr – 24 May
Birdland
By Simon Stephens
Cast includes: Andrew Scott
A piercing new play looking at
empathy, money and fame.

13 Jun – 5 Jul
Co-commission with Center Theatre Group
Adler & Gibb
By Tim Crouch
Tells the story of a raid – on a house,
a life, a reality and a legacy.

17 Jul – 9 Aug
Co-produced with Headlong
The Nether
By Jennifer Haley
An intricate crime drama
and haunting sci-fi thriller.

Jerwood Theatre Upstairs

27 Mar – 3 May
Co-produced with Clean Break and Royal
Exchange Theatre Manchester.
Pests
By Vivienne Franzmann
Pink loves Rolly. Rolly loves Pink.
And Pink loves getting bombed off
her face. The story of two sisters
from the same nest.
Part of the Royal Court's Jerwood New
Playwrights programme, supported by the
Jerwood Charitable Foundation.

11 – 28 June
Co-produced with
Birmingham Repertory Theatre
Khandan (Family)
By Gurpreet Kaur Bhatti
A warm and funny play about
tradition and ambition.

Innovation Partner

Flight Partner

Tickets from £10
020 7565 5000
www.royalcourttheatre.com

■ royalcourt ■ theroyalcourttheatre

Supported using public funding by
**ARTS COUNCIL
ENGLAND**

ROYAL COURT SUPPORTERS

The Royal Court has significant and longstanding relationships with many organisations and individuals who provide vital support. It is this support that makes possible its unique playwriting and audience development programmes.

Coutts supports Innovation at the Royal Court. The Genesis Foundation supports the Royal Court's work with International Playwrights. Theatre Local is sponsored by Bloomberg. Alix Partners support The Big Idea at the Royal Court. The Jerwood Charitable Foundation supports emerging writers through the Jerwood New Playwrights series. The Andrew Lloyd Webber Foundation supports the Royal Court's Studio,which aims to seek out, nurture and support emerging playwrights. The Harold Pinter Playwright's Award is given annually by his widow, Lady Antonia Fraser, to support a new commission at the Royal Court.

PUBLIC FUNDING
Arts Council England, London
British Council
European Commission Representation in the UK

CHARITABLE DONATIONS
Martin Bowley Charitable Trust
Columbia Foundation Fund of the London Community Foundation
Cowley Charitable Trust
The Dorset Foundation
The Eranda Foundation
Genesis Foundation
The Golden Bottle Trust
The Haberdashers' Company
The Idlewild Trust
Jerwood Charitable Foundation
Marina Kleinwort Trust
The Andrew Lloyd Webber Foundation
John Lyon's Charity
Clare McIntyre's Bursary
The Andrew W. Mellon Foundation
The David & Elaine Potter Foundation
Rose Foundation
The Royal College of Psychiatrists
Royal Victoria Hall Foundation
The Sackler Trust
The Sobell Foundation
John Thaw Foundation
The Vandervell Foundation
Sir Siegmund Warburg's Voluntary Settlement
The Garfield Weston Foundation

CORPORATE SUPPORTERS & SPONSORS
AKA
Alix Partners
American Airlines
BBC
Bloomberg
Café Colbert

Coutts
Fever-Tree
Kudos Film & Television
MAC
Moët & Chandon
Quintessentially Vodka
Smythson of Bond Street
White Light Ltd

BUSINESS ASSOCIATES, MEMBERS & BENEFACTORS
Annoushka
Auerbach & Steele Opticians
Bank of America Merrill Lynch
Byfield Consultancy
Capital MSL
Cream
Lazard
Vanity Fair
Waterman Group

DEVELOPMENT ADVOCATES
John Ayton MBE
Elizabeth Bandeen
Kinvara Balfour
Anthony Burton CBE
Piers Butler
Sindy Caplan
Sarah Chappatte
Cas Donald (Vice Chair)
Celeste Fenichel
Emma Marsh (Chair)
Deborah Shaw Marquardt (Vice Chair)
Tom Siebens
Sian Westerman
Daniel Winterfeldt

Supported by

Innovation Partner

INDIVIDUAL MEMBERS

MAJOR DONORS

Eric Abraham
Ray Barrell & Ursula Van Almsick
Cas Donald
Lydia & Manfred Gorvy
Richard & Marcia Grand
Jack & Linda Keenan
Adam Kenwright
Miles Morland
Mr & Mrs Sandy Orr
NoraLee & Jon Sedmak
Deborah Shaw & Stephen Marquardt
Jan & Michael Topham
Monica B Voldstad

MOVER-SHAKERS

Anonymous
Christine Collins
Jordan Cook
Mr & Mrs Roderick Jack
Duncan Matthews QC
Mr & Mrs Timothy D Proctor
Ian & Carol Sellars

BOUNDARY-BREAKERS

Katie Bradford
Piers & Melanie Gibson
David Harding
Madeleine Hodgkin
Philip & Joan Kingsley
Emma Marsh
Edgar & Judith Wallner
Mr & Mrs Nick Wheeler

GROUNDBREAKERS

Anonymous
Allen Appen & Jane Wiest
Moira Andreae
Mr & Mrs Simon Andrews
Nick Archdale
Charlotte Asprey
Jane Attias
Elizabeth & Adam Bandeen
Dr Kate Best
Sarah & David Blomfield
Stan & Val Bond
Neil & Sarah Brener
Deborah Brett
Mr & Mrs William Broeksmit
Joanna Buckenham
Lois Moore & Nigel Burridge
Louise Burton
Clive & Helena Butler

Piers Butler
Sindy & Jonathan Caplan
Gavin & Lesley Casey
Sarah & Philippe Chappatte
Tim & Caroline Clark
Carole & Neville Conrad
Andrea & Anthony Coombs
Clyde Cooper
Ian & Caroline Cormack
Mr & Mrs Cross
Andrew & Amanda Cryer
Alison Davies
Roger & Alison De Haan
Matthew Dean
Polly Devlin OBE
Rob & Cherry Dickins
Sophie Diedrichs-Cox
Denise & Randolph Dumas
Robyn Durie
Glenn & Phyllida Earle
The Edwin Fox Foundation
Lisa Erikson & Edward Ocampo
Mark & Sarah Evans
Celeste & Peter Fenichel
Margy Fenwick
Deborah Ferreira
Beverley Gee
Nick & Julie Gould
Lord & Lady Grabiner
Jill Hackel & Andrzej Zarzycki
Carol Hall
Stephen & Jennifer Harper
Mr & Mrs Sam Haubold
Gordon & Brette Holmes
Kate Hudspeth
Damien Hyland
Suzie & David Hyman
Amanda Ibbetson
Melanie J. Johnson
Nicholas Jones
Dr Evi Kaplanis
David P Kaskel & Christopher A Teano
Vincent & Amanda Keaveny
Peter & Maria Kellner
Nicola Kerr
Steve Kingshott

Mr & Mrs Pawel Kisielewski
Mr & Mrs David & Sarah Kowitz
Rosemary Leith
Imelda Liddiard
Daisy & Richard Littler
Kathryn Ludlow
Beatrice & James Lupton CBE
Suzanne Mackie
Dr Ekaterina Malievskaia & George Goldsmith
Christopher Marek Rencki
Mrs Janet Martin
Andrew McIver
Barbara Minto
Takehito Mitsui
Angelie Moledina
Ann & Gavin Neath CBE
Clive & Annie Norton
Georgia Oetker
James Orme-Smith
Mr & Mrs Guy Paterson
Sir William & Lady Vanessa Patey
William Plapinger & Cassie Murray
Andrea & Hilary Ponti
Annie & Preben Prebensen
Wendy & Philip Press
Mrs Ivetta Rabinovich
Julie Ritter
Paul & Gill Robinson
Andrew & Ariana Rodger
Corinne Rooney
William & Hilary Russell
Julie & Bill Ryan
Sally & Anthony Salz
Bhags Sharma
The Michael & Melanie Sherwood Charitable Foundation
Tom Siebens & Mimi Parsons
Andy Simpkin
Anthony Simpson & Susan Boster
Andrea Sinclair & Serge Kremer
Paul & Rita Skinner
Mr & Mrs RAH Smart
Brian Smith
Barbara Soper
Saadi & Zeina Soudavar
Sue St Johns
The Ulrich Family
Amanda Vail

Constanze Von Unruh
Ian & Victoria Watson & The Watson Foundation
Matthew & Sian Westerman
Anne-Marie Williams
Sir Robert & Lady Wilson
Mr Daniel Winterfeldt & Mr Jonathan Leonhart
Martin & Sally Woodcock
Katherine & Michael Yates

With thanks to our Friends, Stage-Taker and Ice-Breaker members whose support we greatly appreciate.

FOR THE ROYAL COURT

ENGLISH STAGE COMPANY

Become a Member

The Royal Court has been on the cutting edge of new drama for more than 50 years. Thanks to our members, we are able to undertake the vital support of writers and the development of their plays – work which is the lifeblood of the theatre.

In acknowledgement of their support, members are invited to venture beyond the stage door to share in the energy and creativity of Royal Court productions.

Please join us as a member to celebrate our shared ambition whilst helping to ensure our ongoing success. We can't do it without you.

To join as a Royal Court member from £250 a year, please contact Anna Sampson, Development Manager:

Email: annasampson@royalcourttheatre.com
Tel: 020 7565 5049

www.royalcourttheatre.com

The Pass

John Donnelly's plays include *Bone* (Royal Court Theatre), *Corporate Rock* (Nabokov/Latitude Festival), *Conversation #1* (The Factory/V&A/Latitude Festival/ SGP), *Songs of Grace and Redemption* (Liminal Theatre/Theatre 503), *Encourage the Others* (Almeida Lab), *Burning Bird* (Synergy/Unicorn Theatre) and *The Knowledge* (Bush). His version of Chekhov's *The Seagull* was staged by Headlong in 2013.

also by John Donnelly from Faber.

BONE
SONGS OF GRACE AND REDEMPTION
THE KNOWLEDGE
THE SEAGULL (after Chekhov)

JOHN DONNELLY

The Pass

ff

FABER & FABER

First published in 2014
by Faber and Faber Limited
74–77 Great Russell Street
London WC1B 3DA

Typeset by Country Setting, Kingsdown, Kent CT14 8ES
Printed in England by CPI Group (UK) Ltd, Croydon CR0 4YY

A CIP record for this book
is available from the British Library

978-0-571-31403-4

2 4 6 8 10 9 7 5 3

To Frances Grey

and with thanks to

Russell Tovey
Lu Kemp
Tim Stark
Rob Swain
Joe Hill-Gibbins
Nathaniel Martello-White
Jessica Raine
Morven Christie
Dominic Cooke
Dr Henrietta Bowden-Jones
Anna Kessel
Dr Andrew Hill
Dr Teela Sanders
Lisa Foster
Chris Campbell
Vicky Featherstone
Holly Race Roughan
Lisa McGrillis
Gary Carr
Nico Mirallegro

and especially, the eternal Terrier,
John Tiffany

Characters

The Text

Actions and pauses etc. on the whole
should be inferred from the text.
These are occasionally specified for clarity.

A slash / indicates the point at which
the following cue begins.

THE PASS

'My past is everything I never managed to become'

Fernando Pessoa
The Book of Disquiet

One

A hotel in Bulgaria.
  A twin room.
  Portable CD player and portable speakers. A TV.
  A couple of sports bags, contents spilling out.
  Jason, seventeen, in his underwear. He skips with a
rope. Like a boxer. He is sweating.
  The shower is running.
  The hotel phone rings. Jason lets it ring out. The phone
rings. Jason answers it.

Jason Say again?

What? Someone jumping?

No. No no

Try next door. Alright, ta ta

He hangs up. He picks up a towel. Dries himself. Folds
the towel. Lays it on one of the beds.
  He checks his phone, rests his other hand inside his
underwear, looking in the direction of the shower.
  He turns on the television. Flips channels. Slows
down by porn. Moves on. News. War. Sport. Mutes
the sound.
  He plays a CD through the portable speakers – the
music isn't what we were expecting.
  He crosses to one of the sports bags, unzips a side
pocket, pulls out a tub of protein powder and a water
bottle. Unscrews the tub, removes a measuring spoon
and dollops some of the powder into the bottle. He
disappears into the bathroom with his bottle, leaving
the tub uncapped.

He turns the sink tap on. A howl of protest – the voice of another young man.

Ade (*off*) Fuck's sake!

Jason returns, takes a teaspoon from a tray of tea, coffee and packets of biscuits. He eats all the biscuits, stirs the mix, replaces the lid on the bottle, shakes the bottle, removes the lid and exits on to the balcony out of view, drinking the protein shake.

Ade, seventeen, appears in the bathroom doorway, naked apart from a small crucifix on a chain round his neck, drying his groin with a towel.

The shower stops. Jason returns, finishing the last of the shake. He belches, drops the bottle on the floor, performs press-ups.

Ade disappears back into the bathroom. Jason stands, picks up the rope. Skips.

Ade returns, wearing underwear, drying his hair with his towel.

Ade You playing music now?

Jason Can't sleep with the shower on

Ade It's part of my preparations

Jason Well, it woke me up

Ade Was you sleeping?

Jason No

Ade turns off the music. He climbs into bed.
Jason stops skipping, turns the music back on.
Ade sits up. He picks up a copy of a high-end magazine for footballers and flicks through it. Stops.

Ade I want a watch like that

Jason Worth more than your nan's house that is

Ade tosses the magazine aside. He watches Jason skip.

Ade We turn the light out?

Jason I'm awake now

Ade moves to the trolley. No biscuits. Jason stops skipping. Ade returns, slaps Jason's arse.

(*Squeezing his own crotch.*) Squeeze my plums, madam?

Each time they say 'squeeze my plums' it is in a strange high-pitched voice, a shared joke.
Ade wrinkles his nose.

Ade You guffed?

Ade turns the music off. He grabs the remote from the other bed. Flips through channels. Jason picks up the discarded football magazine. Flicks through, one hand down his underwear.

Jason Said you was going to bed

Ade Reckon they got dirty stuff?

Jason Shows up on the bill, that does

Ade Free ones don't

Jason Free ones are shit

Ade Not here they're not. Get anything here

Ade turns the sound on. It is loud.

Jason Steady, someone phoned about the noise

Ade From the club?

Jason No, no, reception

Ade Was you wanking too loud?

Jason Yeah, in your shoes

Ade turns the TV down until it is inaudible. He finds some softcore pornography. He picks up the protein tub.

Ade You take my protein mix?

He looks for his water bottle. Sees it discarded where Jason left it.

You do anything to this?

Jason Might've dangled my winkle in it

Ade spoons out some of the mix, is about to tip it into the bottle, then thinks better of it. He takes the flask and the mix into the bathroom. We hear the tap turn on. Ade emerges, stirring his drink.
Ade stands, watches porn, stirring his drink. He sniffs it uncertainly. Rocks back and forth, miming taking someone from behind.

Ade That toilet is suspect

Jason What you done, you dirty man, you ruined the shitter?

Ade Nah, man, the sensor

Jason What about it?

Ade Goes off when you don't expect. Every time you lean forward it gives your balls a shower

Jason Your plums get a bashing?

Ade Don't like doing a shit with wet balls

Jason Your plums get mashed up?

Ade Wanna see 'em?

Jason Show me your plums, madam?

Ade Squeeze my plums!

Jason Mashed plums, madam!

Ade Mashed plums for tea!

Jason Looks like your sister

Ade No she don't

Jason Does from this angle

Ade I'm turning the light out

Jason You being mother?

Don't turn it out. I get scared

Ade Can't sleep anyway

Ade crosses to the fridge, opens it.

You check out the minibar? Beers, Coke, juice, wine. They got beer, shall we have a beer? Shall we?

Jason If you fancy it

Ade Think I should have one? Jase, Jase, shall I have a beer? Shall I?

Jason Up to you, mate

Ade Ohhh, sweet

He holds up a bottle of champagne.

Jason Have to pay for that now

Ade Ain't gonna drink it

Jason Got sensors, charge you for moving it

Ade No they don't. Really? Fuck off

Jason Let's have a gander

Ade passes the champagne over.

Ade They got johnnies, man. They charge you for these an' all?

Jason Not if you put 'em back

Ade Imagine that, finding a johnny, some guy's jazzle in it

Jason Stop, I'll pop my cordial

> *Ade exits into the bathroom. Jason examines the bottle of champagne. He mimes spraying it as you would celebrating a victory. Ade returns wearing a hooded bathrobe and slippers. Jason puts down the champagne.*
>
> *During the following, Ade fetches a tub of Nutella from his bag. He licks clean the spoon he used for protein shake and eats Nutella direct from the jar.*

Jason Alright, darling

Ade It's like my niece's kitten, this. What you think, shall I take it?

Jason Definitely charge you

Ade What about slippers?

Jason Nah

Ade How come you can take slippers but not a dressing gown?

Jason It's the rules innit. It's very regimented the world of towels

Ade How come you know this?

Jason Holidays

Ade You stay in places like this?

Jason All the same, innit

Ade I never been abroad

Jason What, not even to the motherland?

Ade Nah

Jason Not enough sensors in the bogs for yer?

Ade Nah, they all shit in huts

We didn't even need a passport. You notice, that is like VIP?

Jason You need a passport

Ade We went straight through

Jason Kelly's got 'em. Remember that form we filled in?

Ade Was that our passport?

Jason She looks after them for us

Ade Would you do Kelly?

Jason Nah

Ade Why not?

Jason Probably would actually

Ade What?

Jason That ain't gonna help you sleep

Ade Can't sleep if I'm hungry. Don't trust all this gyppo food, it's suspect

Nan said I should have something English, remind me of home

Jason Nutella? Nutella ain't English

What's it say?

Ade Made in Italy

Still reminds me of home – what? What you laughing at?

Jason You look like an Eskimo

Ade An Eskimo?

Ade speaks in an indistinguishable accent.

Me likey fish! Me eaty plenty fish. Me trappy fish with spear

Jason What is that?

Ade I don't know how Eskimos talk

Jason Eskimos, oh right

Ade leaps up on to Jason's bed. Jason is laughing.

Ade Me trappy plenty fish with spear. Kill fish. Eaty fish with chilli sauce and french fries

Jason Chilli sauce?

Ade Chilli! Chilli monster!

Ade bounces on Jason's bed, spearing and eating imaginary fish. He stands above Jason.

Jason You know how Eskimos kiss? They rub noses. Like that. Or their tongues get stuck together. 'Cause of the cold. Straight up

I can see your billy bollocks

Ade I'm bored now

Ade steps off the bed, enters the bathroom.

You got to the end of Grand Theft Auto yet?

Jason Yeah, finished it, you?

Ade Nearly

Jason End's the best bit. We could chuck that telly out the window?

Something to do

Ade emerges without his dressing gown, brushing his teeth.

Ade You need some pussy, man

Still ain't done my scripts. Should be asleep by now. Imagining the interviews I'm gonna give

Jason Interviews, hark at Doris!

Ade I heard if a lady journalist got a deadline for interviews, they'll give you shines. In the mixed zone after a game, they got a deadline and no one'll talk, some of them'll suck you off, seriously

Jason Where d'you hear that?

Ade Jojo? What?

Jason moves to the bathroom, enters.

Jason Make a lovely couple you two, who makes the tea?

Ade Jealousy is an ugly trait

Jason Milky just how you like it

Ade walks on to the balcony, looks out. He is visible.

Ade (*shouting*) I will fuck you all with my big dick!

Jason emerges, brushing his teeth.

Jason (*laughing*) Shush!

Ade plays coquettishly with the curtain, wearing it as a veil.

Ade Seen the view?

Jason View. Old dears on the other side get a view, we got a building site

Ade How come they get a view?

Jason 'Cause they're regulars. They get the mountains

Ade I want the mountains

Jason We all want the mountains, darling. Come in, it's freezing

Ade Where is Bulgaria?

Jason Europe

Ade Not an idiot, what's it next to?

Jason Be in the pack

Ade That's what I want man. Room with a view

He enters the bathroom. We hear him rinse his mouth and toothbrush. He emerges, takes the skipping rope.

How come you always skipping?

Jason Helps me think

Ade What you think about?

Jason The human condition, Ade

Ade Them girls hanging around the lobby. Some of them is buff

Jason One of them looked like your sister and all

Ade Shut up about my sister yeah, I don't like it

You know Danny and Leesy took a couple of them up to their room?

Jason Did they?

Ade They gave one of them security guys some money to send 'em up

Reckon we should get some?

Jason Go on then

Ade We could get a bird, take it in turns

Jason Your treat?

Ade They ain't prossies

Jason What are they then?

Ade Poison pussies

Jason Poison pussies! Who come up with that? Don't tell me, JoJo

Ade You don't like JoJo

Think he'll play?

Why not?

Jason He don't look up

Ade He hits the ball clean

Jason Can't control it though

Ade That guy's left foot, man

Jason Thinks he's Roberto fucking Carlos. Hits the target about as much too

Ade JoJo reckons they're plants

Jason What, like asparagus?

Ade Like special agents, got their entire own agenda. Want their home team to win so they come here to have sex with us

Jason I'm enjoying this theory

Ade When you come that's your energy, everyone knows that

Jason What PE syllabus did your school do?

Ade Look, I didn't go no posh school

Jason Succubus

Ade Suck your bus?

Jason It's classical. Succubus. A spirit that drains your energy by having sex with you

Ade That's what I'm talking about! Succubus!

Just 'cause I didn't do Latin

Jason Neither did I mate, Class Civ

Ade What's that?

Jason The study of Classical Civilisations. You know, Julius Caesar. Pompeii. Gods turning into swans and shagging people

Ade Believed you till the last bit

Jason Got an A. I was teacher's pet

Ade I don't need GCSEs

Jason You sure?

Ade Look around you, man, they ain't paying for this for a laugh

Jason This ain't nothing to them

Ade Playing a bunch of farmers, course they gonna play us

Jason Some of them farmers can play

Was you watching them videos?

Ade I'm bringing my A-game

Jason Ain't much use on the bench

Ade We ain't gonna be on no bench

What's wrong with you, man, why you think we're here?

Jason Experience

Ade Experience? You been at the Academy since you was what, ten?

Jason Eight

Ade It's a pyramid. All them other kids, but we keep going. Look around you, man, from that original group it's just us and JoJo, the three of us. Champions League!

Jason We already qualified, he's just resting the senior pros

Ade Nah, man, this is it. I'm telling you. Ain't no room for passengers

Jason crosses to the bathroom. He spits and rinses.

I got a little something to show you.

Jason Is it Little Ade?

Ade delves into his bag and produces a smallish video camera (c. 2002). He presses buttons, searching for a section of video. Jason crosses to the balcony window, peers out.

Ade Check this out. Come on, check this out. JoJo and Leesy tag-teamed these girls in Blackburn

Jason No no no, I don't want to watch JoJo's sorry arse bobbing up and down

Blackburn? Jojo wasn't playing

Ade Nah man, stiffs

Jason They picked up a couple of birds they was in the stiffs?

Ade Said they was in the first team

Jason Such unruly boys

Jason sits on Ade's bed, next to Ade. They watch the video.

Who you with?

Ade Vodafone

Jason What deal you on?

Ade Watch, man

Jason My dick's bigger than his

Ade Maybe it's a grower not a shower . . . / Nahhh!

Jason Nahhh!

They laugh. Ade scrolls forward on the video.

Ade This is boring, she just plays with it . . .

Jason Where you get the camera?

Ade My auntie went to America. They got everything there

This is it, this is it, this bit kills me

They listen. Jason bursts out laughing. They laugh, nudging and jostling each other.

Jason 'You ain't gonna show this to no one!'

Ade That is classic, man

Jason You seen his missus?

Ade Leesy's, yeah, man

Jason You feel bad for her?

Ade Man's got urges, she must have known that when she married him

Jason He's always dipping his willy somewhere he shouldn't be. How come it never gets in the papers? He don't even try and hide it

Ade He's got a deal with them

Jason A deal?

Ade Yeah, he told me. Like, if he does something naughty, then his agent phones them up and says, 'You run this dirty story, I ain't gonna let you talk to any of my other clients for six months, but . . . you keep this under wraps, I'll give you a nice interview with Leesy, plus an interview with Becks,' or whoever?

Jason Leesy's got the same agent as Becks?

Ade Nah, I'm just giving an example. I just mean like the big names

Ade crosses to the bathroom, enters.

They don't give a shit what the story is as long as they can sell papers, that's what Leesy says. If you got a story you want to keep out the papers, all you got to do is find another story. They need to keep you onside in the long term 'cause they know you shift papers

Jason So what happens when they do print stuff?

Ade Time to get a new agent

Jason Is that what agents do?

Ade Contracts, image rights and that

Emerges with moisturising cream which he applies to his body.

Your agent not tell you this?

Jason My dad handles all that

Ade Wanna get yourself a proper agent, mate

You got a celebration? Oh I forgot, you never score any goals

Jason That's funny, you should write that down

Ade points to his eye.

Ade See that

Jason See what?

Ade That

Jason What's that?

Ade That's my celebration

Jason That?

Ade I'm gonna trademark that, so I can put it on my merchandise

Jason Looks like you got a bit of dirt in your eye

Ade Ten years from now little kids is gonna be doing that

Jason Are they, Ade?

Ade Yeah, you wait

What?

Jason You black boys, always moisturising

Jason points the camera at Ade.

Ade I don't mind if a girl ain't got a good face if she got a fit body. What was the name of that girl you pulled in that club?

Jason Echoes? That was a shithole

Ade Deano was sharking her all night and you went straight in under his nose. He was well pissed off

Jason He did my nut in in training, kicked the ball straight at me then gave me a row for not controlling it, front of everyone

Ade That how come you banged her? To get back at him?

Jason Can't lose face, can you?

Ade What was she like, man? Come on. She have a tight pussy?

Was it shaved? You go down on it, man, you lick her out? You lick out that tight hot pussy till she cream in your face?

Jason I ask you a question Ade?

Ade Is it dirty?

Jason How do you square your all-consuming hunt for minge with your Christian faith?

Ade What kind of question's that?

Jason Just giving you some practice for all them interviews you're doing

Ade Yeah yeah

Jason Sort of thing Garth Crooks might ask you on *Football Focus*

Ade Black warrior prince needs his pussy

Jason Black warrior what?

Ade Black warrior prince, don't you forget it

Jason Likes talking about it

Ade What you saying?

Jason I'm saying he likes talking about it

Ade More pussy than you

Jason Been checking?

Ade Shut up, ignorant white man

Jason I wouldn't worry, Ade, I'm sure your dad's covered you with a blanket of prayer

Ade Sweet, make fun of my dad

Jason He's a nutter, you said it yourself

Ade He's my dad, alright

Jason 'Do you know Jesus, Jason? Do you know him in your heart?' Straight off the bat

Ade Don't start

Jason 'Hello Mr Lotomo.' 'Do you know Jesus?'

Ade Alright, alright

Jason What was it he said? If there is sin in your –

Ade 'If there is sin in your heart, cast it out'

Jason That's it!

Ade 'How can a man outrun the devil if the devil is in your heart!'

Jason Blimey, he went on. Longest grace I ever heard. Time he'd finished my tea was cold

Ade Imagine living with him

Jason You believe that though?

Ade Some of it

Jason Do you pray?

Ade Yeah

Jason What for?

Ade You should try it

Jason Don't you fucking dare

Ade What?

Jason Don't you try and convert me

Ade I'm just saying, man

Jason I know you too well, I know what you're like, you're a closet nut

Cracks me up, your dad

Ade He likes you, man

Jason Telling me I had the devil in my heart

Ade That's his way. Means he respects you

Jason He ever tell you you had the devil in your heart?

Ade Are you recording this? Don't, you'll wipe over the tape

Jason What, Jojo's skanky home porn, that's a loss to world cinema

Ade Stop pointing that at me, man

Jason Should get some shut-eye

Jason rises, turns off the main light, chucking the camera on Ade's bed.

Ade Keep the small ones on

Jason So you feel safe?

Jason crosses to the balcony, looks out.

Ade What you reckon to Deano?

Jason If Deano was a lolly he'd lick himself to death

Ade Last week after drills we was in the shower and everyone was talking about the squad, yeah, and we didn't know we'd be in it. So he's talking to me: 'Don't worry, this is how it was for me, I know I'm all this and all that now but when I was starting I was in your shoes so don't sweat it, I know what it's like'

And before I'd thought, this guy's a prick. Always in your face in training, giving you a little kick, having a word

Jason Yeah

Ade But he's asking me about myself, taking an interest

Jason Yeah

Ade So now I'm thinking, this guy's actually alright

Then I notice everyone else laughing

He's pissing down my leg

All the time we're talking. He's pissing down my leg in the shower

Jason He's like that with everyone

Ade He piss on your leg?

Jason No

Ade I think he's a bit racist, man

Jason Deano, nah?

Ade Well, not racist, but things he says

Jason exits to the bathroom.

Jason Gives everyone a hard time

Ade He don't piss on everyone's leg, man

Jason It's a sign of affection

Ade Affection?

Jason Yeah, it's cultural

Ade He's from Portsmouth

Jason I never been to Portsmouth

Jason has a piss. Ade watches.

You take these things too personal. He'd take the piss out of you for being ginger.

Ade I ain't ginger

Jason No, no, I mean he's a wind-up, you know, like if you was fat or –

Ade Saying I'm fat now?

Jason No

Ade Look at that, man, that is raw muscle

Jason You got a lovely bikini body, Ade, don't worry

Ade He never passes it in five-a-side

Jason Told me he rated you

Ade He say that? When?

Jason appears to be finishing his piss.

Jason On the coach, when we was playing cards

Ade Did he?

Jason Yeah, he's taken a shine to your style of play

He gets a second wind of piss.

Ade You winding me up?

Jason Straight up

Ade He's played against some good players

Jason The next Bergkamp, that's what he said

Ade You're lying, man

Jason finishes his piss and turns to face Ade.

The next Bergkamp?

Jason He said, 'That Ade, I think he's better than Dennis Bergkamp.' Or was it Dennis Wise?

Ade Fuck you

Jason The black Dennis Wise, that's what he called you

Ade Funny, you should be on telly

Jason I will be, mate

Jason disappears from sight. We hear the tap run briefly.

Ade closes his eyes. He talks quietly under his breath – his 'scripts'. As he does so, he shimmies and feints, receiving and releasing the ball, taking a shot, scoring.

Ade Pass and move. Pass and move. Pass and move. Drop. And go. Drop. And go. Pass and move . . .

He continues the refrain.

Jason emerges from the bathroom, crosses to his kitbag, takes out a pair of football boots and a shoe shining kit. He lays his boots on top of a magazine and, during the following, polishes them methodically.

Jason What you think of that session? Ade? Coach kept switching us inside out

Ade Just drills

He continues the refrain.

Jason Said he wasn't sure I had what it takes, you believe that?

You believe that, Ade?

Ade I'm doing my script

Jason Why you think he said it? Ade?

Ade I don't know, maybe it's 'cause you're quiet

Jason What you mean, 'quiet'?

Ade I'm doing my script, man

Jason What you mean, 'quiet'?

Ade Sometimes you get this look. Like you zone out, like when you skip or shine your shoes or just look out the window

Jason So, what's wrong with that?

Ade Nothing, I just think some people don't get you

Jason Has someone said something?

Ade Coach don't pick the team, yeah, he's probably just trying to motivate you. You worry too much. It's all about the moment, that's all that counts, everything else you can't control

Jason Look behind there's nothing to find / look ahead you're dead

Ade Look ahead you're dead

Coach is funny, man

This ain't the stiffs, they do that for you

Jason I like the smell of polish

Ade Get you hard, does it?

Jason Not as hard as your sister when she sits on my face

Ade I told you, man

Jason Not like the other girls, Ade. She special?

Alright, alright

I think she likes me though

Ade How come you do that?

Jason Helps get me in the zone. Something my dad did. It's his kit. Every Saturday, Dad'd lay his paper down, put the telly on, polish his boots in the front room. Mum'd go spare

Ade He come to all your games, don't he?

Jason Every one

Ade In his Jag?

Jason One of 'em

Ade How many houses he got?

Jason Don't know. He's a builder, it's what he does

Ade My dad's always too busy with his sermons

Jason He come to that festival you was in

Ade Just my nan and my sister

Jason You was good in that. What was that thing you did, you had that red material, you pulled and it kept on coming and you did that . . .

Ade It was abstract movement. It represented – what's so funny?

Jason Nothing, I was just remembering it

He performs a brief gesture approximating his memory of Ade's dance.

Nah, it was good

Ade I liked doing that. I was surprised you come

Jason Course. Why wouldn't I?

Ade No one else did

Jason Give us a blast. Go on

Ade Can't just do it to order

Jason Too much pressure?

Ade throws a pillow at Jason. Ade exits into the bathroom, pulling the door to, but not fully closing it. We hear Ade piss.

Make sure you wash your hands

Jason picks up Ade's tub of Nutella. During the following, Jason smears Nutella on his face.

34

Ade How you know how to play cards?

Jason What's that, mate?

Ade On the bus, you was playing with the older lads? Did your dad teach you?

Toilet flushes. Then we hear the tap.

Jason He used to win my pocket money back off me

Ade What?

Jason He'd give me my pocket money then we'd play cards, he'd win it back

Ade No way

Jason Said it was a lesson in life

Ade Serious?

Ade emerges from the bathroom. Jason attempts a Nigerian accent.

Jason Ade. It's me, Babatunde

Ade What the fuck, man?

Jason Your long-lost brother from Nigeria

Ade Are you kidding me?

Jason Come here, Ade. Show some love to your brother

Ade Get the fuck away from me

Jason tries to hug Ade, Ade shoves him off.

Jason Ade, why you treat me so harshly? I have come so far to see you. It is me, Babatunde, your brother from Nigeria you did not know you had

Your father had many children

Ade Seriously, what the fuck?

Jason Tell me why are you so sad to see Babatunde

Ade marches into the bathroom closes the door.

Jason Ade, Ade

Come on mate, I'm having a laugh

So it's alright for you to talk about gyppos but I can't have a laugh?

Don't be a woman. Fuck's sake. Just a bit of banter

Jason wipes a section of Nutella from his own face. Licks his finger
   Ade emerges from the bathroom smeared with white moisturising cream
   A moment. Ade parades around in an approximation of a cockney.

Ade Awright geez! Awright me old diamond! Me old china!

Jason Babatunde!

Jason performs a cod African dance. Ade turns the music up loud – 'Can You Feel It' by The Jacksons – and performs a cod 'Knees Up Mother Brown'-style cockney dance. They shout Africanisms and cockneyisms. They grab each other, smearing Nutella on one another. Dancing, playfighting, rolling on the bed.

Ade That's my balls, man! I got Nutella on my balls!

Ade sits astride Jason. Ade has pinned Jason's hands down with his legs. Jason makes half-hearted attempts to push him off. Ade pulls his underwear aside and dunks his balls in Jason's mouth. Jason thrashes around. Ade jumps off and flies to the other side of the room in hysterics. Jason wipes his mouth.

Jason Oh you dirty black man, I tasted your chocolate salty balls

Ade (*sings*) Put 'em in your mouth and suck 'em!

Jason crosses to Ade, gives him a dead arm.

Okay, enough, enough!

Jason I'm never having Nutella again, that is rank

The phone rings. A moment. They laugh.

Ade I ain't answering it

Don't don't don't don't

Jason answers the phone in his cod Nigerian accent. Ade turns the music off.

Jason My name is Babatunde, how can I help you?

I apologise, I am meeting my long-lost brother Babatunde

Ade Thought you was Babatunde

Jason And we are performing traditional Nigerian dance in celebration

No. It won't happen again

I am sorry for inconveniencing you and I will put monies in your bank account as compensation goodbye

Jason hangs up. He and Ade crack up laughing.

Ade You're mad, man, you're fucking mad!

Is this is a bit racist?

Jason Nah, just shits and giggles

Ade That was funny as fuck

How'm I gonna sleep in that?

Jason Looks like we smeared shit everywhere

Ade You know Babatunde's my dad's name?

Jason Is it?

Ade picks up a discarded bathrobe and walks out on to the balcony.

Where you going you doughnut?

Come back

I'm all alone!

Ade appears, his face a death mask, white with the cream, his robe open, revealing him to be naked underneath, genitals tucked between his legs.

(*Laughing.*) What the fuck!

Ade uses the gauze from the curtain as a veil. He performs a simple gesture. A more elegant version of the one Jason performed earlier – its source in fact. Jason laughs.

Wally

Jason enters the bathroom.

Ade My dick keeps twitching

What you talk about when you're playing cards?

Jason You on about that again?

Jason emerges, wiping off Nutella with a towel.

It's sort of a rule – you're in the game or you're not

Ade What you mean?

Jason You have to pay to play. What goes on in the game stays in the game. Like Vegas

Ade Come on, man, don't be a dick, what you talk about?

Jason collects shower gel from his bag.

Seriously? Alright, did you win, you can tell me that?
Come on, how'd you do?

Jason Don't really work like that

Ade Someone got to win or lose

Jason You're up or you're down, it goes in a book

Ade So you lost

Jason No, I was *down*

Ade Getting touchy is she?

Jason I'm just saying, you know nish about cards

Ade 'Cause you're the big man now

Jason Didn't say I'm the big man

Ade 'I play cards with the big boys'

Jason Well, I didn't notice the big boys inviting you into their game

Ade That's 'cause I ain't a mug

How much they take from you?

Jason Told you, that's not how it –

Ade Scared I might laugh?

Jason A monkey

Ade A what?

What's a monkey?

Jason makes a monkey noise.

Jason Oo-oo-oo

Five hundred. It's slang. Five hundred

Ade A monkey's five hundred?

Jason Yes

Ade Pounds?

Jason Yes, Ade, pounds, English pounds, five hundred pounds

Ade You lost five hundred in two hours, that's your wage, mate

Jason No, I was down five hundred in two hours. Next week I might be up, that's how it goes, you played cards, you'd know that

Ade If you're playing

Jason What?

Ade If you're playing next week

Jason What's that supposed to mean?

Ade Just saying you might not be playing

Jason We both might not be playing

Ade Oh, I'll be playing

Jason Saying you're better than me?

Ade Let's just drop it, alright

Jason No, no, I'm intrigued. Oh, actually, no, it's alright I understand

Ade What?

Jason I understand

Ade What, what do you understand? You don't understand nothing, you're just saying it to seem all mysterious like you know something

Jason Pressure's getting to you

Ade Pressure's getting to me?

Jason Making you act up

Ade I ain't the one messed up today

Jason What you talking about?

Ade What you think?

Jason That was your fault

Ade My fault?

Jason You really want to do this?

Ade You were supposed to be marking him

Jason You were supposed to be covering

Ade It was your zone

Jason I'd pushed up

Ade It was your zone, that was the point of the session

Jason We were playing on the overlap, that means my man becomes your man, vice versa. Every time before, I pushed on, you dropped back

Ade So I pushed up that time

Jason I was already up

Ade Wasn't me who Coach shouted at, alright?

Jason I know. I know it wasn't

Ade What was I supposed to do?

Jason Not go flying up when I'm already up, leaving us open at the back

Ade It was only a training game

Jason I'm just saying in the game don't leave me looking like I lost my man

Ade And I'm saying in the game don't lose your man

He moves past Jason to the bathroom door.

Jason When you're playing overlap, and I push on, my man becomes your man. Where you going, don't fucking walk off in the middle of this, where you going?

Ade I'm going for a piss, alright

Jason We're talking, don't just walk off

Ade I'm having a piss, that alright?

Jason Yeah, it's alright

Ade Just so you know, I'll be leaving a space that side of the room, you think it's too big, you might wanna push up and cover it

Jason Next time you fancy a shot at glory, leave me staring at my own arsehole, how about you give me a bit of advance notice, you cunt?

Ade They was laughing at you. Deano, Leesy. Laughing about taking your money at cards, how you think you're one of the boys

Jason Bollocks

Ade They said they thought you was a bit suspect

Jason When was this?

Ade When you was in the shower

Jason How you mean?

Ade Different

Jason Different, what's that supposed to mean? What's that supposed to mean?

Ade A bit – you know

Jason No, I don't know

Ade Posh

Jason Posh? Posh! I'm from Stanford Le fucking Hope!

Ade You ain't exactly from the ends

Jason I'm having a beer

Ade Cracking up, is it?

Let's not pretend we don't know what's going on. We got eight months left on our contracts, they gonna let one of us go they're doing it soon, else they get nothing. They can't keep us both on, not with this new formation

Jason I know that, Ade, I'm not thick

Ade There's a window, yeah, I can see it closing

Jason If I'm in a better position tomorrow and I'm on, will you pass me the ball?

Ade, I'm asking you a question

Ade When your chance comes you best take it, yeah? 'Cause that's what I'm gonna do

Maybe I just need this more than you

Look, it ain't nothing personal. It never is

Jason Really?

Jason goes to the fridge, takes a beer, opens it, drinks.

This is stupid

Whatever happens, we'll always be brothers, yeah? Come on, mate

Here

Ade We got a game tomorrow

Jason You turning me down? Ade, you gonna leave me hanging?

Ade? Brothers

Ade drinks. Passes it back.

Ade Brothers

Jason drinks.

Jason Doughnut

Jason gives Ade a playful punch. Ade gives Jason a punch back, slightly harder. Jason returns harder still. Ade bundles Jason on to the bed.

Ah yes! Yes! Don't stop! Ah! Ah yes! Wanna squeeze my plums?

Ade You fucking bender, I'll feel your plums!

Jason He does an' all! Ooh matron, that's rather pleasant – what the fuck was that?

Jason pulls away looking shocked. Ade is still laughing.

Ade I squeeze your plums!

Jason Seriously, what the actual fuck?

Ade What? We was, we was . . .

Jason You had a fucking hard on. You did, you had a hard-on

Ade No I didn't

Jason You did, mate, I felt it. You had a fucking hard-on

Ade No, I . . .

Jason You did

Ade I get nervous

Jason Well I ain't keeping this to myself

Ade Please, man

Jason I'll be telling everyone about this

Ade I just get nervous before a game

I get nervous

Please, it was just

Jason I'm pulling your leg. I'm pulling your leg, Ade. Loads of people get a hard-on before a game, I know I do. I get a massive hard-on

Ade Do yer?

Jason Yeah, course

You alright? You look scared

Ade Why would I be scared?

Jason Give us a cuddle, you bumboy

Ade moves towards Jason. Jason gives him a deep cuddle.

You're very huggable. Ade, you know that?

Ade Piss off

Ade shoves Jason off. It's playful. Jason looks Ade square in the eye. Gives him an Eskimo kiss – rubs noses with him. Strokes his cheek. Gives it a couple of gentle friendly slaps.

Jason Doughnut

Jason walks to the shower. Turns it on. He reappears.

Ade. I'm gonna take a shower now

Jason returns to the shower. He leaves the door open. Ade stares, frozen.

Two

A hotel in Spain.
  Double room.
  A TV and entertainment system, including iPod dock.
  A dresser. On which, a handbag.
  Champagne on ice.
  *Lyndsey, twenty-nine, on the balcony, looking out. She
wears a light summer dress*
  She steps on to the bed and bounces

Lyndsey You have a trampoline when you were a kid?
My friend did, it was lethal

  *Jason, now twenty-four, emerges from the bathroom.
He is dressed for a warm summer evening out. Fetches
himself a beer from the minibar. As he passes, Lyndsey
drags him up on to the bed. He removes his shoes first.
They bounce a little together.*

See

  *Jason climbs down. He turns the TV on. Turns the
volume down low. A Spanish-language* culebrón (*soap
opera*) *plays.*

Jason Just a bit of background, take the edge off

  *Lyndsey comes down from the bed, tries to lead Jason
to the balcony.*

Lyndsey Come and look at Africa

Jason Africa? This is Spain

Lyndsey See those lights over the water? That's Morocco

Jason Yeah, I know

Lyndsey Love watching boats at night

Jason moves to the balcony. He and Lyndsey are close. She pulls the curtain over her face, making a veil, a playful gesture. He moves to the fridge.

Jason Drink?

Lyndsey Sure

Jason picks a bottle of champagne from the fridge. Glasses. Starts to open the champagne.

It's weird how hotel rooms feel like they've always been yours. Six twists. It's always six twists with the wire. A sommelier told us that. Must see a lot of hotel rooms?

Jason Yeah

Lyndsey They lost their magic?

Jason opens the bottle. Pours.

I like your eyes. I'm actually jealous of your eyelashes. I was thinking that in the club

What part of your knee is it? In the taxi, you were talking about your knee

Jason It's my meniscal cartilage

Lyndsey Dancers get that. You try coming down off a pole in six-inch heels. Ballet's the worst, all the jumps. I used to want to be a ballerina

Jason What happened?

Lyndsey Got tits

Jason I saw Aurélie Dupont in *La Sylphide* in Milan a couple of years back

Lyndsey Aurélie Dupont?

Jason We had a game at the San Siro. Normally you can't hang about after an away game, but I was being rested for a cup tie so I stayed on. She was alright

Lyndsey That's one way of putting it

Saw it happen, your knee. On telly I mean, oh God, all different angles

Jason Alright!

Lyndsey Sorry, people tell us I talk too much, if I'm talking too much just tell me to shut up I won't be offended. It's what my sister does. Actually when it's her I do get offended, but that's 'cause we just never got on. Do you want me to shut up?

Jason My knee's fine, cheers

Lyndsey Cheers. Can I just do something? Do you mind?

Jason Do I have a choice?

Lyndsey Not really

Lyndsey reaches out and presses her palm flat against his stomach.

I been wanting to do that all evening. Your abs are actually amazing, go on, don't be shy.

He lifts his shirt up.

Honestly, are they drawn on? Ah, you can smile

Sorry, I'm doing it again, it's second nature. Your patter, I mean, you got to talk to the customers, interest them in a dance and –

Jason Right

Lyndsey Like some of them just want a straight flirt. You know, in another life they might actually have a chance. You get the odd dick likes to act all superior so you have to laugh at their jokes and pretend you don't notice when he takes the piss out of you to his mates. And some of them, they want to get to know the real you, you know, sincerity's their thing. It's like role play. (*Responding to Jason raising an eyebrow.*) Cheeky!

This one guy, regular customer, lovely man, he was so supportive about me doing my degree, amazing tipper. When I dropped out, I didn't have the heart to tell him, so I pretended I was doing all my exams and whatnot. Two years I kept that going, he wanted to come to my graduation, had to fob him off, say I could only get tickets for family

People just like to be friendly, you know, like they're not taking advantage

Jason You enjoy it?

Lyndsey Plenty worse jobs. I get to choose my own hours, great tips, on a good night I can make some decent money

Jason Bad night?

Lyndsey On a bad night, you end up with less money than when you walked in the door, yeah. Once you factor in the taxis and the overheads

Jason Overheads?

Lyndsey These nails don't maintain themselves, darling. Plus there's the house fees. I mean you have to pay to dance. You pay the house at the start of the night, then you have to earn that back to break even. That's why you need your patter. Got to make hay while you can, always someone younger looking over your shoulder

Jason Yeah

Lyndsey Though I reckon you probably make a bit more hay than I do

Jason I reckon I do too

Lyndsey You're confident. I like that in a man

I shouldn't be telling you this, I'm giving away my trade secrets. That's always been my problem, I'm too open

Jason You don't seem like a normal stripper?

Lyndsey What did you call me? Did you just call me a stripper?

Jason Why, is that . . .

Lyndsey Stripper my arse, I'm a table-dancer

Jason I didn't mean nothing by it

Lyndsey Do you want me to fucking brain you? Seriously? D'you see me with a pint glass collecting change? Stripper! Strippers stick their tits out and sway, I'm an artist, pal! That mouth of yours'll get yourself in trouble you're not careful

Jason Alright, okay

Lyndsey Stripper! But you're right, I'm not like the other girls. Between you and me, some of them are thick as shite, seriously. Nothing up here. I mean for me this is just temporary. Don't get us wrong, I enjoy it, but it's just part of my ten-year plan

Jason You got a ten-year plan?

Lyndsey I'm gonna dance for a while, save enough to get a deposit on a flat, maybe finish my degree

Jason How come you left?

Lyndsey Started doing this. There was proper money in it back then, grand a night, I mean you probably laugh at that, but, you know. I mean this was to pay my student loan, but you get used to a lifestyle and . . . Picked up a few silly habits, started hanging out with the wrong people. Hindsight's a wonderful thing

Jason What you study?

Lyndsey Business. It's great, you get a bit of everything, economics, psychology

Jason I could have gone to uni

Lyndsey Never too late. You meet all sorts of different people. Opens you up, especially coming from the kind of place I grew up. You know, gives you a sense of what life has to offer, though that can have its downsides

Jason How so?

Lyndsey Some things will always be out of reach for some people

Jason *E em torno de mim todos poentes incógnitos douram, morrendo, as paisagens que nunca verei*

Lyndsey Is that Spanish?

Jason Portuguese

Lyndsey What does it mean?

Jason 'And all around me, dying, unknown sunsets brush with gold, landscapes I will never see'

I played in Portugal for a year. Germany too. I speak three languages. Does that surprise you?

Lyndsey I think you'd like it to

Jason You're good though. At the dancing. You move well actually

Lyndsey It's harder than people think

Jason What, dancing round a pole?

Lyndsey What, kicking a ball?

She approaches. Stands close to him.
    Pushes him down on the bed, stands astride him.
    Takes his hand. Moves it on to her thighs.

Lyndsey Go on

Jason What?

Lyndsey Give them a squeeze

I'm serious

Jason squeezes Lyndsey's thigh.

Jason They're not bad actually

Lyndsey Fuck off, *not bad*, they're fantastic. Beyoncé can do one

'Not bad'! Fucking twat, you're asking for a slap

Jason Like the rough stuff?

Lyndsey Don't think I won't, I do kickboxing

Jason Ooh

Lyndsey You're not how I thought you'd be either. I thought you'd be less . . .

Jason Intelligent

Lyndsey Shy

Jason What do you mean, how you thought I'd be?

Lyndsey When Victor introduced us. You know that photo of you and him is going to be up on the club wall? And the girls were talking about you while we were waiting to go on. I mean, I didn't know who you were. If I'm honest, I find football quite boring. I've said something wrong, haven't I? Honestly, ignore me, sometimes I just say what comes into my head. The girls were so excited though. There was a little more lip gloss than usual applied tonight

Jason What did they say about me?

Lyndsey The girls. They said you're very good. Are you?

Jason Yeah

Lyndsey The general consensus was you're quite fit

Jason Quite?

Lyndsey They also said you were very modest

Jason That's true too

Lyndsey Must be amazing knowing you can do something better than anyone else in the world. Do you wake up in the morning all, like, 'I am *really* good at football'

Jason Mostly I think about what I could do better

Lyndsey Must be great though. All those people singing your name

Jason Depends what they're singing

Lyndsey Can you hear what they say?

Jason Quieter grounds you can, you know, bigger clubs, when they got fans just there for a sandwich. Throw-ins and corners when you're right near 'em, someone shouts 'I hope your kid dies of cancer,' you hear every word

Lyndsey People say that?

Jason You switch off. Or you use it, you know. To motivate you. That's not always a good thing though

Lyndsey How come?

Jason Sometimes you don't think logical when your blood's up

Lyndsey Do other players say stuff?

Jason Normally stuff about shagging your missus, that's standard. Your kids is off limits though

Lyndsey There's an etiquette to calling someone a cunt?

Jason Yeah

Lyndsey What? What's that grin?

Jason Just now you said you hadn't heard of me

Lyndsey I'm sorry, that was a really dumb thing to say

Jason Well, before you said you saw me do my knee on telly, so I –

Lyndsey Well, I mean I know who you are, I just didn't know you were – I'm just not a fan, you know, like . . . D'you know what I mean? Am I making sense? Honestly, don't listen to me, I just talk shite half the time, I really do. I mean, yes, I do know who you are. I just didn't want to make a thing of it. I just imagine you get that all the time, people being all – Oh, you're kidding us on, aren't you?

Jason Yeah

Lyndsey Very good

Jason You really do kickboxing?

Lyndsey What, you think I lie about everything now?

Jason Do you though?

Lyndsey And a bit of aikido, aye

Jason Go on then

Lyndsey No, Jason

Jason What?

Lyndsey No no no no no

Jason Why not?

Lyndsey Men always ask this, it always ends in tears

Jason Ask what?

Lyndsey What you really want to know is could I put you on the ground. Why have men got such a thing about that? Is it 'cause you're in charge all the time so you like being dominated by a woman, you know, see how it feels? Yes, Jason I could put you on the ground, but let's not go there

Jason Oh, you're backing down

Lyndsey I'm not backing down, I'm just saying it's not a good idea

Jason Course you couldn't, you're a bird

Lyndsey Stand there

Jason Ooh, stand to attention

Lyndsey I'm not mucking about, over there

Jason Why there? Why not here? Or here? Or here?

Lyndsey 'Cause I don't want you to hit your head on the way down

Jason Ooh, she's confident, this one, she's confident

Lyndsey Hold your arm out

Jason Why, we gonna dance?

Lyndsey And your hand like that

Jason Oh, I'm getting nervous now, I'm ah ah. Fuck my balls. Fuck my balls. Fuck my – ah ah –

Lyndsey takes Jason's wrist, turns his arm over and apparently without much effort she forces him to his knees and then down on to the floor. She steps away. Jason rubs his hand.

That was a good one, you nearly had me there

Lyndsey I did warn you

Jason How'd you do that, there's nothing to yer

Lyndsey My ex was the instructor

Jason Now you tell me! Anything else I should know?

Lyndsey What's that?

Jason What?

Lyndsey That, down there. Oh it's your self-esteem

Jason Nice, good banter, yeah

Lyndsey helps him up. They are very close.
They kiss. Jason gently extricates himself.

Going for a piss

Jason exits into the bathroom.

Lyndsey Mind if I smoke?

Jason No, go ahead

Lyndsey goes to her bag. She takes out a pack of
cigarettes and a lighter. Lights one.
She adjusts the bag so that one edge of it is in line
with the bed, facing it.
Jason enters. Lyndsey is still smoking.

Lyndsey Bit of a luxury this, can't do it back home any
more

Jason You live on your own or –

Lyndsey With my mum. I know. Just came out of
something, sort of in between things? Hoping to get a
place of our own, somewhere with a garden but the
deposit's a bastard

Jason Who's we? You said 'of our own'? Like there was
someone apart from you and your mum. What, like a
fella or –

Lyndsey My son. He's nearly eight

Jason Must have had him young

Lyndsey Aye, I did. You okay with that?

Jason Yeah

Still, I suppose your mum can help out

Lyndsey You've not met my mum. I need my own space, you know, I don't think that's too much to ask

Jason Council not sort you something?

Lyndsey No fucking way. No son of mine's growing up the kind of places I grew up. No way

Jason Think you'll manage that, the deposit?

Lyndsey I'm working on it

Jason Your mum know what you do?

Lyndsey Yeah

Jason She okay with that?

Lyndsey Well, it's not every mother's dream, is it? We're just different. She worked forty years doing shit jobs and has fuck all to show for it. Stuck in a shit marriage with my dad till he left her. I love her but she's so small-minded. Just had this mentality of being happy with your lot. I mean, why should you be happy with your lot? Other people are rich. They don't work harder than I do, how come they get to have all the nice stuff? I like nice things. I want nice things. Why shouldn't I have a nice car or a nice house just because I was born in the wrong place?

Ah, Mum's okay really. It's my sister who's the pain in the arse. Two years older, she's the golden child, you know, never gets anything wrong. Chartered surveyor. Nice house, nice garden, two really boring kids. So boring. She's a wee bit sniffy about me, you know, like I'm letting the side down or something. You know, how about a bit of female solidarity? Sees herself as a bit of a feminist, you know

Jason My cousin's a feminist

Lyndsey Is she?

Jason Went off to uni, come back one

Lyndsey It can do that to you, university. Think it's the high concentration of public schoolboys

Jason You're not one of these women think all men are wankers then?

Lyndsey All men *are* wankers! I don't mean it in a bad way, it's not your fault, you just are. Don't get us wrong, I love men. I mean, mostly you're harmless wankers, but you're still wankers. I almost feel sorry for you. Like I love my son to bits. I would do anything for him, but some of the things he comes out with, I'm like, Jesus, it's started. He's already showing the signs of arseholedom. Seven years old

Jason Is that why you do it, for your son?

Lyndsey Do what?

Jason Dancing

Lyndsey Oh, 'cause that would make it okay? I danced before I had Scott, it's nothing to do with him. Like I say, I like the freedom

Jason I've got a son

Lyndsey Okay

Sorry, d'you mind if we don't talk about this? It's just if you talk about someone it sort of brings them in the room, and I don't want my son in the room

I'm sorry, this probably isn't the conversation you had in mind when you invited us back

Jason I ask you something?

Lyndsey Go ahead

Jason Are you playing a role now?

Lyndsey How d'you mean?

Jason Before you said you had your patter, you know

Lyndsey I don't follow

Jason That you'd play a role, are you doing that now with me?

Lyndsey I'm not at work now

Jason So this is the real you?

Lyndsey Okay, let's clear this up. I don't go off with customers, that's not what I'm paid for

Jason Isn't it?

Lyndsey I dance. That is it. Let's not muddy the lines. Apart from anything else, it's not good for business

Jason What makes me so special?

Lyndsey Who's to say you are?

Jason, come on, pet. I'm not stupid, I saw your wedding photos in *OK*

Let's not make things more complicated than they are. I'm here the same reason as you. I'm bored and lonely and away from the things I know. And sometimes it's nice having someone to ease the pain. Even if it's just for an hour or two

We're two people in a room. Tomorrow someone will come in and clean this all away. Fresh soap, fresh towels, fresh sheets

Or have I misjudged the situation?

Jason No

Lyndsey Maybe it's the situation that's making you tense

Jason I'm not tense

Lyndsey Jason, you're like a jack-in-the-box, getting all paranoid

Jason I'm not paranoid

Lyndsey Says the man who's not paranoid

Jason Don't tell me I'm paranoid

Lyndsey Okay, okay

Look, there's no pressure. We don't have to do anything

Jason Don't we?

Lyndsey Let's just talk, okay?

Jason Talk?

Lyndsey Yeah, you know, like people

Jason What about?

Lyndsey What do you do to relax? Like before a game

Jason Why you asking me that?

Lyndsey I thought you might find it relaxing to talk about what you find relaxing

Jason I don't need to relax

Lyndsey Or maybe we could do the thing you find relaxing?

Jason I told you I don't need to relax

Lyndsey Okay. Sorry

Jason I do my script. To relax

Lyndsey Your script?

Jason You visualise things you do, in the game, rolling your man, shaping to move. Play it out, like a tape, see yourself do it all

Lyndsey Like a fantasy

Jason Your brain can't tell the difference between something you make up and something you remember, so when the real thing comes up, you don't have to think, it's all there, is this interesting to you?

Lyndsey It is

Jason The idea is to make everything seem familiar 'cause unfamiliar things distract you. So you're always in the moment. That's what nerves are, it's to do with something that's about to happen. Making a decision. Once you made the decision, you're laughing, that's when instinct kicks in

You get the weirdest dreams the night before a big game

Lyndsey What, the one where you're naked in front of people? I get those before I start a new job, only in mine, it's the other way round, the audience is naked and I'm all layered up

Jason Well, in mine, I'm in a game where the formation keeps changing. Everyone around me's so fluid and it's like I'm stuck

Lyndsey Funny things nerves

Jason Affect people in different ways

Lyndsey How do they affect you?

Jason Sometimes you feel tired. Or angry. Sometimes you get horny

Lyndsey Is that so?

First job I had dancing was in a sports bar, you know they had girls dancing while they showed the games on big tellies. I've always been confident about my body but still, when it's strangers, it's not like a doctor or you know . . . And as I took my top off, first time I done it, a big cheer went up. And I thought it was for us, but it was the football. Someone had scored a goal

Jason They was watching the game?

Lyndsey It really pissed me off

Jason I wouldn't have watched the game while you was on

Lyndsey Thanks. Anyway, I wasn't nervous after that

Jason They call that displacement. If you think about the thing you're doing too much it stops you doing it

Lyndsey I find that with anything physical

Jason First game I played. European game. Usually someone'll try and give you an easy touch early doors, put you at ease, but our centre back won possession, knocked it to me. And at that level it's fast, so much less time on the ball than you're used to

The ball comes to me and I hesitate. And their man must sense that 'cause straight away he's closing me down and the pass I want isn't on. So just on instinct really, I stepped over the ball, slid a pass out left. And a little cheer goes up from the away end, 'cause it looked cheeky you know, like I was taunting him. And that was all I needed

Not long after, ball comes out near the bye line, I meet it, at pace. Straight away, defender's on the back foot, now he's already on a card, so he don't want to slide in. So I shift my weight and I'm away. Now there's a pass on. My mate. His first game too. He's probably in a slightly better position all told, and because of that, he's drawing a man. And I just think, it's on. I should pass, but something in me

So I skin their centre back, and in doing that, I've pushed myself wider than I want, the shot's on but the angle's not great. My mate now, he's screaming, and really I should pass, 'cause now I'm being closed down and he's lost his marker. But I don't. I hit it. Sort of shot that can fly into Row F. But that confidence. And it's stupid 'cause that feeling can be misleading but this time. Fuck me, I caught it sweet

And that little cheer I told you about. Well this was a roar. You can barely take it in, it's this heat almost, you can't breathe. Time goes a bit wobbly. All your team-mates pile on. Fucking hell, I'm welling up thinking about it

Lyndsey What happened to your mate?

Jason Some people just aren't cut out for it. Under the lights they sort of seize up. And you can't tell until you're out there. Get the cockiest sods in the world, they can't do it. Then some lads are like fucking church mice and you see a different side to 'em

Lyndsey Must be hard, finding out you aren't good enough

Jason If you're gonna get found out, better sooner than later. Since age eight, it's all you've ever known then at sixteen or whatever

Lyndsey Eight?

Jason My dad had me doing timed shuttle-runs up and down the garden when I was five

Lyndsey Did you like all that?

Jason I liked winning. Least, I hated losing. And if you don't want to lose you have to put the hours in. Talent is bullshit. It's all about what you're willing to sacrifice. Most people think football's all blood and guts and hard tackles and that but really it's about space. Controlling it. Finding it. All the movement, you see, it's about one thing. Finding the space. That's why good players look like they got all the time in the world. 'Cause they found the space

Lyndsey moves to Jason. They kiss. It becomes passionate. They begin to undress.
   Lyndsey calls a halt.

What you doing? Where you going?

Lyndsey I thought I could do this but I can't

She gathers her shoes. She wants to get to her handbag. Jason blocks her way.

Jason What you mean?

Lyndsey Can I get my bag please?

Can I get my bag please?

Jason What you mean, you thought you could do this?

Lyndsey D'you want a fucking stiletto through your eye? I mean it, my bag

Jason picks up the handbag, holds it out of her reach.

Jason What you want the bag for?

Lyndsey It's my bag, moron. It's got my passport

Jason That all?

Lyndsey You want an inventory? Tampons, lipstick, tissues

Jason What else?

Lyndsey Well, there might be some bits of fluff and a toothbrush, is that okay?

Get out the way or I will batter you

I mean it, you'll get this through your fucking eye

I'll call the police

I don't want any trouble, okay, just give us the handbag and I'll go

What are you doing, you nutter?

Jason empties the contents of the bag on to the floor.
They are pretty much as described.

Jason Where is it?

Lyndsey Where's what?

Jason The camera. The camera you're using to record this

Lyndsey Are you out of your mind?

Jason There's a camera in here, I know there is, don't lie to me

He turns the bag upside down, shaking everything out.

Lyndsey You are actually starting to scare me now, you are actually starting to scare me. I'm calling the police

Jason Fine, call the police

Lyndsey I'm calling them

Lyndsey takes her phone, dials a number.

Paranoid fucking mental case, is this what happens when you get famous, you turn into a cunt, lose your mind?

Jason It's here somewhere

Lyndsey Mental. Fucking crazy man. I pity you. I'm just imagining your wife's face when she hears about this, bet she'll fucking love it

What will she think? What will your wife think?

Jason Don't talk about my wife

Lyndsey Oh what, big man, shouting at me?

Jason I'm not shouting

Lyndsey Used to that are you, that how you talk to your wife?

Jason Where is it?

Lyndsey How long does it fucking take them to answer? Got her trained, have you, like a little doggy

Jason Don't talk about her –

Lyndsey Little lapdog, yap-yap-yap

Jason I said –

Lyndsey Or what, you'll hit us?

Jason No

Lyndsey That it, you'll hit us, that how you treat women, that what you're used to? I am going to laugh when the cops get here. Fucking nerve, looking down on me? I'm not the one with wifey curled at up home, where's your missus, eh? On your leather sofa, with your son, that's where, silly bitch, I pity her, married to a piss artist like you. That's it! Raise your fist to me! (Hello, yes, police please.) At fucking last. Think I'm scared? You're the worst of the lot, come into the clubs, think you're a cut above, not like the other customers, we take your money and we laugh, we fucking laugh, you sorry piece of

(Hello, yes, I'm in the Hotel Excelsior. There's a man, he's threatening me, he won't let me leave)

Last chance

(Yeah, he's right here)

This is your last chance to give me my bag back and let us go

(I'm in the Ocean Suite. Yes please)

Lyndsey ends the call.

Any minute

Any fucking minute

Look, you don't need this, I don't either, just give me my bag, and that's the end of it, I'll go, you can tell the police whatever you like

Jason Try again

Lyndsey What?

Jason Try again

Lyndsey Try again what?

Jason In Spanish. Try phoning them in Spanish

Lyndsey takes a while before she speaks.

Lyndsey I don't want any trouble, okay. Just give us my bag and I'll go

Jason Where is it?

Lyndsey I just want to leave, okay

It's on the side. It's a little –

Jason This it?

Lyndsey Yes

They approached me, it wasn't my idea. These people offered me money. A lot of money. I'm being honest, I'm telling you everything I know. There's a man downstairs, I'm supposed to give him the bag. I don't do this, okay, I've never done this, I swear

Jason You expect me to believe that?

Lyndsey I don't care if you believe it or not, it's true

Don't look at me like that

What, you're just going to stand there?

Fucking say something

Look, you're the one with the wife, okay, not me

Just give us the bag and you'll never see us again, I promise

I'm saying nothing. Nothing happened, I won't say a thing

Jason I know

Lyndsey What do you mean, you know?

Jason I know you won't say anything

Lyndsey How do you know?

Jason 'Cause of what you signed

Lyndsey What do you mean, 'cause of what I signed?

Jason Let's have a drink

Lyndsey I don't want a drink

Jason Let's have a drink and talk

Lyndsey 'Cause of what I signed, what does that mean, how do you know what I signed?

Jason Let's calm down

Lyndsey Don't tell me to calm down

Jason Okay

Lyndsey You knew about this?

You stood there while I justified myself, all the time you knew?

Jason Two minutes ago you thought you was taking me for a ride

Lyndsey Is this something you do, for kicks, make tapes of yourself for your mates, some weird . . .

I want to know what is going on. I don't care what I signed or didn't sign, you tell me what is going on or I am walking out that door

Jason Okay, I believe you, okay

I'm just going to pour myself a drink, and then we'll talk

I'll pour you a drink

Lyndsey I'm not really in the mood for champagne

Jason G and T then

Lyndsey The G on its own is fine

Jason fetches a miniature gin from the minibar. He pours it for Lyndsey. Hands it to her. She downs it in one. He fetches another. She downs the bottle. It takes Jason a long time to speak.

Jason I don't expect you to understand, okay. 'Why?' doesn't matter

Okay, okay, okay

I get money, endorsements, because people think I have a certain image. They buy shirts with my name on it, boots, that sort of thing. It sounds silly but it's very lucrative. And people are telling stories that cause problems for that image

Lyndsey What kind of stories?

Jason It doesn't matter

Lyndsey What kind of stories?

Jason It doesn't matter, the point is they're not true. Remember what you signed

Lyndsey Are you – are you joking us? Are you –

Jason You laughing at me? Are you laughing. Don't fucking laugh

Lyndsey I'm sorry, I can't help it. I'm sorry, I just got the giggles

Jason It's just rumours. It's just rumours, okay

Lyndsey Rumours? You're doing this over rumours?

Jason Do you have any idea the world I live in? How it works?

Lyndsey Whatever

Jason You think I want fifty thousand people chanting stuff, you think I want my kid hearing stuff at school, getting abuse in the street

Lyndsey It's none of my business

Jason You have no idea what you're talking about, you just don't get it

Lyndsey Jason, darling, I just don't think people care any more

Jason Great, I'll base my future financial security on some tart's opinion

Lyndsey Hey. Don't get angry with me 'cause you hate yourself

Jason You don't know anything about me

Lyndsey And you don't know anything about me. You talk to me about security? Take me years to earn what you earn in a week, this isn't about money, this is about people finding out you're, you're gay or whatever

Jason That I'm what?

Lyndsey That you're . . .

Jason Are you out of your fucking mind?

Lyndsey I mean that's what –

Jason Gay? Gay?

Lyndsey Okay, it's none of my business

Jason No love, I'm not gay, what kind of word is 'gay'?

Lyndsey So what are you then?

Jason I'm an athlete. A warrior. I go out and do battle every week in front of a baying mob. I sell millions in merchandise, I embody people's hopes and dreams, I'm not gay. I don't know why I'm even bothering, I can't expect you to get it. You can't begin to fathom the pressure I'm under

Lyndsey Pressure?

Jason So if there are certain requirements that I have to fulfil my role, if there are things I need to carry out that task, if I need to fuck a woman or a man or a fucking apricot for that matter, or have a wife and a kid to come home to, then that is what I do. I live the way I live to do what I have to do. And that is it. I don't know what kind of absurd little reality you live in but that is my world. So, no, love, I'm not gay, that don't even come into it

Lyndsey Okay

Jason No one decides who I am or what I do but me

Lyndsey I get it, alright

Jason No one gets the better of me, not some idiots out there starting rumours, no one. I'm not a man who lets other people dictate the pattern of play!

Lyndsey That's what this is about isn't it?

You didn't need to tell me this

You could have done all this, got it over with, without saying a thing

You needed me to know. Didn't you?

You could have fucked this whole thing because you had to let me know you were smarter than us

That's what this is about, you just couldn't bear the thought of me leaving here thinking I'd got one over on you

You're pathetic. Standing there, like a scared little boy

Jason When you've finished your speech, do you want this fucking money or not?

Lyndsey No

I want double

Oh what? Would you rather I was more reluctant? Would that do it for you?

People do more for less every day. This is nothing special

Who watches these things anyway? Wankers in betting shops?

> *Lyndsey finishes her drink. She sets the camera up (positions the handbag, switches it on).*

Jason Is there sound?

Lyndsey There's no microphone

Have you done this before? With a woman, I mean

Jason I've got a kid

I don't know if I can do this

Lyndsey No, we're doing this. We're doing this, alright. 'Cause I can't afford your fucking reservations

We're not backing out just 'cause you're having some crisis of confidence. So man up. You fucking pansy

> *Jason pours himself a glass of champagne.*

Jason Thanks. Just needed to get my game face on

You're right by the way. None of this is fair. But that's just how it goes, innit? It's only weak people who complain about the cards they're dealt. The rest of us just get on with it

What you want the money for anyway?

Lyndsey None of your business, pet

Jason I'm good at this

Lyndsey Sorry

Jason I should say, I'm good at this. I'm good in bed.
Lots of people have told me

Lyndsey Sure

Jason I know that sounds arrogant, but I am

Lyndsey Whatever, Jason

Jason No, no, I am. I really am. It's not an idle boast

I always have been. Anything physical. I just had a knack

Lyndsey You think I care?

Jason I'm just saying

I mean. No sense us not enjoying it. That won't make no
difference will it?

Three

A hotel in England.
  A suite.
  Jason, now twenty-nine.
  Ade, now twenty-nine.
  Jason is on a spinning bike, cycling.
  A German film plays on a television (for instance,
Warnung vor einer heiligen Nutte *by R. W. Fassbinder).*
  An ice bucket.

Jason You got Grand Theft Auto? The new one?

Ade Yeah yeah

Jason You done all the missions?

Ade Most of 'em

Jason Done 'em all, mate

Ade Have you?

Jason I once spent an entire night just driving round the city, not even doing a mission. Just driving

Ade I done that

Jason It's quite soothing innit? I like to chill out with a nice Scotch and cruise the streets at night

Ade Do yer!

Jason That's a bit sad, innit? Is that a bit sad?

Ade You seen that film? With Ryan Gosling

Jason One where he's a driver?

Ade Yeah yeah yeah, that's what it's called, 'Driver'

Jason *Drive*

Ade That's what I said

Jason No no, *Drive* not 'Driver'

Ade Is it? You sure it's not 'Driver'?

Jason Yeah it's called *Drive*. I love that film

Ade Anyway, that bit where he bashes his head

Jason That's mental

Ade That bit is –

Jason It's mental. He's like, bosh! Bosh! And they're playing that music

Ade He's a really good actor, Ryan Gosling

Jason He is actually a good actor

Ade Like he can just do a look and like –

Jason Yeah he's one of them people he might be looking at something and most people you'd be 'What you doing, you're just staring,' but with him you're like, 'There's something going on, don't know what, but there's something going on'

Ade Yeah

Jason Same again?

Ade Please. You alright having another one?

Jason Course

Ade With the painkillers, I mean

Jason That which doesn't kill you – it's fine, I do it all the time

Saw your website. For your company

Ade You saw that?

Jason Try before you buy

Ade It's alright innit?

Jason Not bad, mate, not bad. Some lovely testimonials. 'Excellent finish', that was from JoJo and his missus

Ade Piss off

Jason You run it with your sister

Ade What, you my stalker now?

Jason How is she, she alright?

Ade Yeah, she's doing good

Jason Say hello from me

Ade Shut up

Jason What, I'm being friendly!

Ade I did that myself actually, that website

Jason The whole thing?

Ade Done a course, when I did my Corgi. PFA give me a loan

Jason Good for something then

Ade No, they were good, I got my GCSEs. Made me wish I'd paid more attention in school, I was just so focused on the one thing, you know

Jason Hindsight

Ade That's it, that's it exactly

Jason I'm so pleased for you, mate

Ade Thank you, thank you

Jason I got a lot of respect for you

Ade Thanks

Jason I been doing a bit of self-improvement too actually

Ade Oh yeah?

Jason The *New Statesman* – it's this magazine –

Ade Yeah, yeah, I know what –

Jason They got this Professor of Economics to interview me, I think they was trying to be ironic or something. So, anyway, we met up a few times and now we have banter on Twitter. He gives me reading lists. Proper books, you know, not like Dan Brown. I love it, winds people up something chronic but that just means more followers

Ade How many you got now?

Jason Nearly a million

Ade Right

Jason Nothing like you think, professors. Thought they'd be all sort of beaky but he's shagging half his students. Think he talks it up to be honest, fancies himself as one of the boys. Apparently, he's quite high up in Marxism. Reckons we only invented civilisation 'cause we needed something to do on the weekend. He's quite lonely, I think. Here, pass us them tubs will you?

Jason stops cycling. Ade picks up the tubs, examines them.

Come on, chop- chop

Ade hands Jason the tubs.

Fetch us a beer while you're at it

Ade What your last slave die of?

Jason AIDS. Help yourself to one and all

Ade takes a beer, passes Jason a beer. Jason gets off the bike.

You still play?

Ade I turn up

Jason Whereabouts?

Ade Marshes

Jason Hackney Marshes! Pitches still shit?

Ade Yeah

Jason What's the standard, any good?

Ade Not really

Jason Bet you're like Ronaldo with that lot, top scorer?

Ade I am quite good actually

Jason Ronaldo of the Marshes

Ade See people's faces when I tell 'em I played with you, no one believes me. Then I show 'em photos

Jason You talk about the old days?

Ade Get bought drinks

Jason My old man used to play there

Ade Did he?

Jason Till he had to start taking me training on a Sunday

Ade How is your old man?

Jason Ah, you know. Less said the better really. I'd love to play Hackney Marshes. Reckon it'd be a laugh, I should turn out for your team sometime

Ade Yeah

How's your knee? I read you had keyhole

Jason The arthroscopy? Standard. Should have done it ages ago, actually had it booked in two years back then they brought this Sierra Leone kid in and I thought, can't take time off now, lose my place. This last knock though, it was getting daft. You know, I'm missing the end of the season anyhow, may as well get it sorted

Ade And it worked?

Jason Yeah yeah, I'm doing conditioning now, no impact yet, put myself in the frame for January. Might have to adapt my game a bit. Ain't the same over five yards, but I got it up here. Go on, you're on

Ade What?

Jason Your turn. See if you can beat my time. If you're up to it

Ade swigs his beer, puts it down. Climbs on the bike. Jason pushes a few buttons. Ade starts cycling.

Ade Hotel alright with this in here?

Jason These prices, they have to be

Ade Haven't they got a gym?

Jason Couldn't be done with the hassle. You know, sweating away on an exercise bike, every two seconds someone wants an autograph for his nephew

Ade Yeah

Jason Makes a good training base this place. Don't get bothered, room service, Michelin-starred chef, cooks what I what. Got a twenty-metre pool too. I got my own key so I use it middle of the night when it's quiet

Ade When d'you sleep?

Jason Honestly, my clock's all wonky. Amount of energy drinks I'm on, I'm up half the night and the painkillers don't help

Ade I swim

Jason I can tell, you beauty

Ade One K, every day

Jason You do tumble turns?

Ade Yeah, yeah, proper turns like on the Olympics

It's quite fun this

Jason Gets harder as you get higher

Ade Higher?

Jason You're in the Alps

Ade The Alps?

Jason You're doing an *étage*, mate

Ade A what?

Jason An *étage*. Tour de France, it's one of the settings. See that dot

Ade Yeah

Jason That's you. See that other dot

Ade One in front?

Jason That's me. You're off the pace already. Working up a sweat I see

Ade Thought I'd put in a shift

Jason Mess your nice shirt up

Ade takes his shirt off. Jason takes it, folds it.

Ade Been here a while then?

Jason Sort of in-between things. You know, Karen got our place as part of the settlement. You know, for her and the kids. Truth be told, I got some interest from other clubs so I don't want to buy anywhere in case I have to move

Ade Where's all your stuff?

Jason Storage. Costs a fucking arm and a leg

Ade Who's showing the interest?

Jason Can't say

Ade Go on

Jason Can't say

Ade Go on

Jason A club in Qatar

Ade What club in Qatar?

Jason They haven't actually been invented yet

Ade You pulling my leg?

Jason They're gonna be part of a franchise, sounds / funny, I know but they're building the infrastructure, paying top dollar to get players in

Ade Mate, Qatar

Jason You laugh! It's like Becks in the States, they're getting their act together, that's where the money is, Guardiola played there

Ade Did he?

Jason End of his career, it's good enough for Pep . . .

Ade So you're saying this is the end of your career?

Jason No

Ade Just banter, mate, you just said it's where Guardiola –

Jason Yeah, I know, keep up, Ade. It's just a bit of leverage really. You know, tell my current chairman I got some interest, see if I can bump my wages up. Giving up already?

Ade Can't be arsed

Jason Where's the dot? Harder than you think innit? Here you go

Ade climbs down from the bike. Jason passes him a towel.

Ade So what's this job then?

Jason What?

Ade Your text, you said –

Jason Fancy another one? Sorry, just noticed you was empty

Ade Uh yeah

Jason Sorry

Ade In your text, you mentioned a job / it's why I'm –

Jason Oh yeah yeah that was it

Ade – something you wanted looking at

Jason fetches an iPad.

Jason Jojo said you did a good job on his place. He said his missus was dead impressed. Have a butcher's at that

You need to swipe with two fingers otherwise –

Ade I have got one, you know

Jason That's one of the new ones

I need it doing up, thought you might be the man for the job. See that's the terrace, it's north-facing so it gets sun all day, it's lovely

Ade Decent

Jason It's alright, yeah

Ade Where is it?

Jason On the Med. Aegean Sea. Nice views

Ade So what you want doing?

Jason Whole thing really. You do that or just plumbing?

Ade I can get people in, but . . . you want someone local, I mean where is it again?

Jason Greece

Ade There'll be a Find-a-Plumber thing for Greece, you know, forums

Jason I need someone I can rely on. I don't speak Greek and I won't have a clue if they're legit or not. Had it a few years, just never really took care of it. Be a nice bolt-hole. Besides, thought I'd bung you some work

Ade Bung me some what?

Jason Some work

If you don't want to do it –

Ade I'm not saying I don't want to do it, I just . . . I don't need you to bung me some work

Jason I just thought it might be nice to do some work in the sun

Ade Jase

Jason Golden sand, blue sky. You can use it while you're out there, have a few mates out. Leave it as you found it

Ade Jase

Jason You can watch the sunrise lying in bed. I could visit

Ade Jase mate, I got a two-month backlog

Jason Well it ain't urgent, I'm just saying, if you want the work

Ade Do you want me to do it?

Jason I just asked you!

Ade I'll do you a quote

Jason That's all I'm saying

Ade That's why you asked me here?

Jason He just said you did a good job, Jojo. His missus was very pleased. Said you did a walk-in shower

Ade I did. It had motion sensors and directional lighting

Jason Eh! Sensors! That was a mad night wa'n'it?

You remember that? Before that game

Ade Oh yeah, yeah, it was a bit, yeah

Jason Lot's changed since then. Married, divorced, two kids. You got your business

Jojo mentioned you was seeing someone

Ade Gary

Jason How's that going?

Ade Yeah, it's alright

Jason Alright?

Ade Well, you know. Been a couple of years now

Jason You live together?

Ade Not yet

We're working out what we want

Jason He watch you play? Up the Marshes

Ade Sometimes

Jason Does he come out for beers with you and the lads?

Ade If he wants to

Jason And does he, want to?

Ade Well, you just get all sorts of in-jokes

Jason I see

Ade It's a bit boring for him. He knows he's welcome

You seeing anyone?

Jason It's hard to meet people, well, you know, people that don't have an angle

Ade Saw about you and that dancer

Jason See the tape?

Ade Some of it

Jason Thought you might have

Ade Must be hard to know who you can trust

Jason Parties I go to these days, almost everyone is off the telly or married to someone you know. It makes the world feel quite small

I was out in LA, you get these parties that are exclusively for famous people

Ade Can imagine!

Jason You have to check your phone in at the door

Ade Serious?

Jason They're all held in these big houses. They all look like this. These days people want their houses to look like hotels

Ade Sounds a bit mad

Jason If you wanted, you could come to one

Ade What, in LA?

Jason If you want

Ade What happens at these parties?

Jason People can talk. Be themselves. They're just parties. Good ones, though

Ade Jason, is there something –

Jason Listen, Ade, I thought maybe we could clear the air

You know, about that night

Ade Right

Jason I mean there's no point, you know

Ade Right

Jason Just thought I'd bring it up, 'cause it's sort of in the air and that kind of thing if you don't talk about it, it builds up into something it's not. Am I making sense, d'you know what I mean?

Ade I think so, yeah

Jason Sort of thing you put too much weight on, 'Oh this thing happened when we was kids,' you know

I'm saying it wasn't a big thing. Unless you feel different

Ade No, I feel the same

Jason Good. I'm glad. So no hard feelings yeah?

Ade Why would there be hard feelings?

Jason Well, exactly, that's what I'm saying. Just good to have all your cards on the table. You know, nothing up no one's sleeve

Ade No surprises

Jason That's what I mean

It's so good to see you, Ade

Ade Yeah. I mean when I got your text –

Jason I mean you can go all psychological on it, but it was just fun and games, you know? Wasn't it?

Ade Yeah

Jason Squeeze my plums!

Squeeze my plums!

Go on. I know you want to. Don't be coy now, Ade

Ade Squeeze my plums!

Jason That's it! Ah ha haaaa! Nice fresh plums!

Ade Mashed plums for tea!

Jason Fresh plums!

Doughnut

Ade Listen, I should be . . .

Jason No!

Ade I got work tomorrow and there's a drive

Jason You only just got here! Ade, we should do something, what's up with you?

Ade Like what?

Jason I don't know, mark the occasion, what's it been, eleven, twelve years –

Ade Twelve

Jason Me and you. Like the old days. You can't go. When was the last time you had a proper blowout? Let your hair down. Come on, what you say, tomorrow's another day. Tonight's about me and you

Ade What you got in mind?

Jason That's it!

Ade I'm just saying what you got in mind?

Jason You're staying, you know you are

Ade You got that look

Jason What look?

Ade Like you used to, when you was gonna do something mad? What? What you thinking?

Jason No, we can't

Ade What?

Jason It's too much

Ade Just say it!

Jason D'you remember we once talked about throwing a telly out the window?

Ade You are joking, mate

Jason Shall we though? Shall we do it?

Ade Can't do that

Jason Why not?

Ade What if it hits someone?

Jason Alright, health and safety! Don't get your knickers in a twiddle

What? You're thinking about it, aren't you? Aren't you?

Ade It has been a while since I done anything really silly

Jason Gary a bit uptight?

Ade No no no, he's just –

Jason Is he though?

Ade No he's just, he keeps me grounded

Jason He sounds awfully fun

Ade No he's just –

Jason Is he a bit sensible?

Ade He can be a bit

Go on then

Jason Ha haa! Yes mate! Right. How'd you do this? You get that side, I'll

They attempt to pull the telly off the wall.

Ade That's going nowhere

Jason Try again. Coordinated effort this time. One, two, three

They try again.

Ade I think it's screwed on

Jason You're screwed on

Ade We need a screwdriver

Jason I thought you was a plumber

Ade I don't just carry 'em round with me

Jason I'll ring down, get room service to bring one up

Ade What, 'Can I have a screwdriver?'

Jason They got everything

Ade Will it not look a bit . . .

Jason Ain't gonna tell 'em why. What? What?

Ade Imagine if you did

Jason What, tell 'em? Shall I? Ade, shall I tell 'em?

He picks up the hotel phone.

Shall I do it? Shall I do it? I'm gonna do it

He dials reception.

Hello, I would like a screwdriver

Ade Make sure it's a Phillips

Jason Phillips-head screwdriver. What size?

Ade Just tell 'em to bring whatever they got

Jason Just bring what you got

Yeah, I need to get the telly off the wall

So I can lob it off the balcony

Yeah, that's right

Yeah

Sweet

Jason ends the call.

Ade That's funny as fuck

Jason That is fucking funny though

Ade 'So I can lob it off the balcony'

What he say?

Jason He said alright!

Ade Did he?

Jason Yeah

Ade He ain't gonna come up, is he?

Jason No

Ade I'm a bit disappointed now

Jason I got quite up for that

Ade I'm quite up for something actually

Jason I am too now. Shall we take some of my pills?

Ade Aren't they for your knee?

What's in them?

Jason Tramadol and temazepam. They're quite fun if you take too many

Ade Is that safe?

Jason Do a job

Ade Alright, but we can't do nothing stupid

Jason Sure sure sure sure

Ade I got to be in London first thing, I'm plumbing in a downstairs loo

Music. The Jacksons' 'Can You Feel It'. Loud.
They destroy absolutely everything.

TWO

Jason and Ade drop balloon bombs from the balcony.

Jason Left a bit, right a bit. One two three

Jason drops a balloon. A pause. They cheer and laugh.

Ade My turn my turn my turn

Jason Keep your panties on

Ade How come you got all these balloons?

Jason Don't know. Said something on Twitter, next thing I know they turned up

Ade lets go of a balloon. A pause. They cheer and laugh.

Ade We mullered this room, mate

Jason Yeah, Ade, I'm sorry, I might have to claim I was robbed by a black man. I'm joking, I'm joking

Ade Come on

Jason I'm joking, mate

Ade That ain't funny no more

Jason How come you're laughing then?

Ade 'Cause I took too many drugs

Jason You ain't took enough by the sounds of it

Ade You don't change, do yer?

Jason Look at you! Look at you!

Ade What?

Jason Standing here all . . . Gaahhhh! It's good to have you back, mate, things ain't been the same without you

Tousles Ade's hair.

It's a shame you didn't carry on. 'Cause you was good.

Ade Thank you. Yeah I was

Jason You was very good. But you seem happy now so that's good too

Ade Yeah

Jason Got a lot of respect for you, Ade

Ade What?

Jason I got a lot of respect for you

Ade How d'you mean?

Jason Working man like yourself

Ade Working . . . ? What's, what's that got to do with anything?

Jason Just saying you're a grafter

Ade A grafter?

Jason Well you know, some people can get stuck on a dream, but you . . .

Ade I what?

Jason Why you being all . . . ?

Ade I'm just asking what that means, you respect me?

Jason Means I – I'm not sure what you're saying, it means I respect you

Ade Yeah, but why say it?

Jason Think you got crossed wires, mate

Ade No I don't think I have. You said it twice now

Jason That's 'cause you're making me repeat myself

Ade No, before. I'm just starting to wonder why you're telling me you respect me?

Jason We was having a laugh

Ade 'Can I bung you some work?' Or you'll grace us with your presence on Hackney Marshes

Jason Oh come on, mate

Ade No, don't 'come on, mate'. What's all that about?

Jason (*Nigerian accent*) Ade!

Ade I ain't making this up. 'Can I bung you some work?'

Jason (*Nigerian accent*) Ade, why so sad?

Ade Don't try and fob this off alright, this sort of shit ain't funny no more

Jason Jesus, Ade what is it you can't handle, the booze or the pills or the failure?

Ade The what?

Jason Oh come on, you're pretty transparent, Ade, let's face it, you was never a complicated man

Ade Think you're so much better than me, don't you?

Jason Oh I see

Ade No, don't say that, Jason, don't say 'I see' like you –

Jason No, no no, it's crystal clear

Ade – got some secret knowledge like all you need to say is 'I see' and it's case closed or something

Jason Ade, I'm sorry things didn't work out, but that ain't my fault

Ade You think that's what this is about?

Jason What, you'd rather be plumbing than doing what I do?

Ade What, cooped up here like a nutter, going for midnight swims in your dressing gown?

Jason Obviously I mean football and for your information, it's a kimono

Ade Oh sorry

Jason You're telling me you don't wish it was you playing instead of me?

Ade Course I do

Jason opens his arms – 'Well then?'

What is that supposed to mean?

Jason You're jealous

Ade Of you?

Jason No, the fucking concierge, who d'you think?

Ade Jason, you're saying this like it's some big revelation. Course I'd rather be playing professional football. Course I would, but that's life, mate. No one gets to do the things they dream about

Jason Except I do, Ade. I do

Ade Well done, I'm pleased, you got lucky

Jason You think it was luck?

Ade Not just luck

Jason I was a better player than you, mate

Ade Bullshit

Jason Ade. I had Milan after me. I was third in the Ballon d'Or. You spend your Sundays in a park in East London trying to nutmeg dog turds

Ade I was stronger, fitter, had better control

Jason And you think that means you was better?

Ade At that time, yeah. Obviously not now, but at that time. Don't pull faces, that is the truth

Jason No, that's right, Ade

Ade Yeah it is right

Jason It is the truth

Ade So you admit it?

Jason I do

Ade You admit I was the better player

Jason Yes you was. You was the better player. You had better touch, pace

Ade Thank you

Jason So much talent

Ade Thank you

Jason All that hard work

Ade Damn straight

Jason And still you managed to fuck it up

Now that's real talent. To be that good, to have the world at your feet then the only moment that counts . . . You bottle it

Ade I did not bottle it

Jason How's that feel, Ade? 'Cause I wouldn't know

Ade I did not bottle it

Jason History suggests otherwise

Ade I didn't get a chance

Jason You had your chance, you didn't take it

Ade How could I have taken it, you didn't pass me the ball?

Jason I didn't need to, Ade, I scored

Ade That should have been my goal, I should have scored that

Jason Here we go, now we get to it

Ade I was in a better position

Jason No, the best position is the one you score from, Ade, that was the position I was in

Ade You said you'd pass me the ball

Jason It's not the playground, Ade, it don't work like that in the big boys' game

Ade That was my only chance, I was subbed off after that

Jason You was subbed off because two minutes later you gave the ball away in our half and they scored

Ade I was taking the man on, it didn't come off

Jason That's why you should have passed

Ade To you?

Jason Yeah

Ade Why would I pass to you when you wouldn't pass to me?

Jason 'Cause I was in the better position!

Ade What, so you could score again?

Jason You lost the ball! You lost the ball and they scored!

Ade Nine times out of ten, I'd have skinned him, I did it in training all the time

Jason We're all George Best in the back garden

Ade Alright, I made a bad choice, I should have passed and I didn't, that don't mean I wasn't unlucky

Jason And why did you make a bad choice, Ade?

Ade 'Cause my mind wasn't in the right place

Jason And why was that?

Why wasn't your mind in the right place?

Ade You know why

Jason Do I? I'm not sure I know what you're talking about

Ade What went on between us?

Jason When?

We discussed this. Thought we agreed it was nothing

Ade You tell yourself that all you like but we both know what went on in that room

Jason What, a handjob? A handjob I gave you when we was kids? You're harping on about a wank you had twelve years ago, Ade!

Ade Wasn't just that

Jason What was it then?

Ade Jase, you put your finger up my arse

Jason Had to put it somewhere. Oh come on, it was only a tickle

Ade, I'd have fucked a penguin at that age . . . I'm sorry if you got confused or –

Ade Confused? You're the one got confused

Jason Alright. Okay? You want to know why I did what I did?

Ade Whatever bullshit you're going to come out with –

Jason I did it to get in your head. Throw you off balance. Make sure you weren't right. For the game

You said it yourself, your head wasn't in the right place, well mine was. The morning after, on the coach to that game, you was sat fiddling with your headphones, shitting it. Me, I was on it, mate, mapping it out

Like you said, I didn't have your pace, or your first touch, but what I did have was this

Taps his head.

I've always had it, a sort of ability to see the gap. The vision to know what needs to be done and do exactly that

What concerns me is that you been hanging on to this fantasy of yours for twelve years, that's, that's not healthy. Does Gary know you're still hung up on this? Or maybe you think of me sometimes when you're with him, spice things up

Ade It wasn't a handjob I got confused about

Jason Right, so it was the finger?

Ade No. It wasn't the finger

It was the way you held me all night. Stroked my hair. Told me I was special

Since we was scholars, we would sit together, room together, we did everything together. But that morning, before the biggest game of our lives –

Jason For you maybe

Ade For both of us. I was waiting on the coach for you. When you stepped on, I looked up at you and smiled. And you walked straight by, didn't even look. I needed to know everything was alright

After, I tried to talk to you, but you was with the other lads, being the big man 'cause you scored, they interviewed you. Next week, squad list goes up, I ain't there. But you was

They didn't renew my contract. I texted, left voicemails, nothing. It was like I was dead

How could you do that? After everything that passed between us

Jason I can't really remember every detail to be completely honest, Ade

And if that is what happened, and who's to say it's not, my memory of it just isn't as strong as yours

Ade Is that right?

Jason A lot's happened since then. I suppose things happen in our lives that mean more to one person than they do to another

Ade You're saying that meant nothing to you?

Jason I'm saying it wasn't the life-defining moment it seems to have been for you, Ade. I've got other things to worry about, rather than some incident than happened in the past

Ade So how come you invited me here? If you got so many other things to think about. How come you asked me?

Jason I could ask you, Ade, why you come? Show me you'd moved on. How'd that work out?

Just to see if you'd come back here. I knew you couldn't resist, just like I knew you was watching me when I made that tape. Feel your eyes on me. Now you're here though. I'm not sure why I bothered

Ade What do you mean, 'come back here'?

Jason What?

Ade You said 'come back here', what you mean?

Jason To this room

Ade I never been here before

Jason I know

Knocking at the door.

THREE

Ade and Jason in exactly the same positions. Harry holds a screwdriver

Harry You asked for a screwdriver

Jason (*We wanted to*) get the telly off the wall

Harry What you want to do that for?

Jason Lob it off the balcony

Harry You'll need an electric, it's drilled in

Ade Okay, well, thanks for the advice

Harry You boys have been busy

Jason How'd you get in here?

Ade You just let him in

Jason Fancy a beer?

Harry Yeah, alright

Ade Probably not when he's working

Harry I'm only supposed to be on till three and it's ten past already

Jason So you're clocked off, are you?

Harry Said I'd do it as a favour

Jason That's very nice of you, I bet you was well brought up

He fetches Harry a beer.

Harry (*acknowledging Ade*) Alright

Jason What's your name?

Harry Harry

Jason Pleased to meet you, Harry

Harry Pleased to meet you . . . Jason!

Jason This is Ade. Say hello to Ade, Harry

Harry Hello, Ade

Jason Ade's shy

Harry What you watching, a porno?

Jason Nah, it's German

Harry You seen *Inception*?

Jason Yeah

Harry That's a good film. Ta

Been doing pills? Your eyes have gone. I won't tell. Work here long enough you see it all

Jason I bet you do, Harry

Harry Thing with hotels, you're running round all day like a blue-arsed fly, clock off at some ungodly hour, but the adrenalin's still there you know, always looking for the party

Jason I bet you can normally find it and all

Harry Yeah, I can!

Jason How about it then? You with us

Ade Is this a good idea?

Harry Go on, how many you normally take?

Jason Start with three or four, see how you go

Harry I'll have double that I reckon. Looks of things I'm playing catch-up

Jason Good man

Ade I think it's time Harry was leaving

Jason Don't be rude, Ade

Harry It's his room

Jason I think Harry should stay. If you want to, Harry?

Harry gets his phone out.

Ade What you doing?

Jason Just wants a souvenir, don't you, mate. You won't put that on social media, will you?

Harry Nah, course not. Will you take a piccy of us?

Jason Don't be a spoilsport, Ade

Harry It's alright, I'll do a selfie

Harry takes a photo of himself with Jason. Examines it.

This is bonkers

Not being funny, right, but when I was younger, that video of you and that lapdancer was a bit of a staple. Went all round my year at school. I put it on once when I was shagging my girlfriend. Took a selfie of me and her, watching you, sent it to my mates. We broke up quite soon after that, I hate girls who haven't got a sense of humour

Jason It's important

Harry They did one of them *Downfall* ones, d'you see that? One of them spoofs, you know with Hitler in the bunker getting narky about owt. 'I cannot beleef you gif me a sex tape wizzout sound!' Her son had something wrong with him, di'n't he?

Jason I don't know

Harry She was well fit. Is that real?

Jason What this? Yeah. You can have it if you want?

Harry Really?

Jason Yeah, go on

Jason gives Harry his watch. Harry puts it on.

Am I the most famous person you met?

Harry Yeah, though a mate of mine met Jimmy Savile. Come to his school. Yeah. This was before it all came out, you know, they wouldn't invite him now, I don't reckon

Ade He's dead

Harry Well, yeah. Listen to this, right. They give him the tour, y'know of the school, and at one point, Sir Jimmy wants a slash. So my mate takes him. Away from everyone. And while they're on their way to the lavs, Sir Jimmy's asking him questions like, 'So what subjects you do? D'you like running?' That sort of thing. Then, when they get to the bogs, out of nowhere, and he swears this is true, Sir Jimmy asks if he can touch my mate's balls

Ade Did he let him?

Harry It's Jimmy Savile! This was before people knew he was a nonce

Jason What happened after that?

Harry Well, at that point my mate thought, something's not right, you know when you get a feeling? Made his excuses. Got a photo of himself though with Sir Jimmy, a normal one, he showed me it. Probably worth a bit now, he should eBay it

Jason What do you think we should do with Harry, Ade?

Harry I'm up for anything really, my mates say I got no boundaries. I'm one of them people can just drink and drink and I don't get drunk. I get that from my dad. Don't get hangovers either

Jason Remember them days, Ade?

Why don't we play a game?

Harry What, like a drinking game?

Jason I bet you know some, you look the sort

Harry I do actually, loads. D'you know Forfeit or Dare? Or is it Dare or Forfeit? What is the difference between a forfeit and a dare? Oh fuck it, anyway, it's a good 'un

Jason He's funny, isn't he? You're funny

Harry Am I?

Jason Yeah

Harry I am actually

Ade I don't think this is a good idea

Jason What do you think, Harry? You think Ade should stay or go?

Harry Think it's up to him

Jason Up to you

Ade This is batshit, mate, this ain't normal

Jason Normal!

Harry I could get some birds in? Give my girlfriend a call, she can bring her mates, they like to party

Ade Jason, what you doing?

Jason No one's making you stay, Ade

Ade I don't think it's a good idea I leave

Jason You my chaperone?

Ade I ain't playing no drinking games

Harry No, no, you stay you play, come on, that's the rules. Stay you play, mate, come on

Jason He's right, Ade. Stay you play. No room for passengers

Ade considers this. Begins to leave.

Misplace your nerve again?

Ade stops.

Ade Don't think I don't know what you're doing

Jason Tell me, Ade, what am I doing? What am I doing? / What am I doing? What am I doing? What am I doing? What am I doing?

Harry A-de! A-de! A-de! A-de! A-de!

Ade Will you shut the fuck up?

Jason Your call, Ade. But either way, let's make a decision, I'm growing a beard here

FOUR

A series of silly drinking games. Increasingly narcotic, competitive, aggressive and terrifying. Everyone joins in.

FIVE

Ade, Jason and Harry, all with trousers round their ankles. Ade and Jason line up. Harry holds a balloon aloft, solemnly. Harry lets go of the balloon. Ade and Jason race from one end of the room and back again. Shot

glasses line the route. Each time they reach a shot glass, they neck the shot. Jason and Ade sabotage one another en route.

Ade wins.

Harry I proclaim Ade the victor!

Harry lifts Ade's arm aloft. Jason acknowledges the victory. Harry presents Ade with a bottle of vodka. Ade does a victory dance to gloat. He is in Jason's face. Jason brushes him away, visibly annoyed. Harry eggs Ade on, goading Jason too. Jason waves him away a few times, but Harry persists. Jason grabs Harry, forces him to the ground.

Jason Pass us that bucket, come on. The bucket. Empty this in it.

Ade fetches the ice bucket, pours the bottle of vodka into it. Jason shoves Harry's face down into the bucket.

Drink up! Drink up!

Jason lets Harry come up for air.

How you doing, Harry, you alright?

Harry Yes thanks

Jason shoves Harry's head straight back down into the vodka. Forces him to drink. Ade laughs. Jason lets Harry up for air.

Jason Alright?

Harry One more

Jason shoves Harry's head straight back down. Forces him to drink. Ade laughs. Jason lets Harry up for air.

Actually, I can't breathe –

Jason shoves Harry's head back down. Ade laughs.
Harry starts to cough and splutter. It goes on too long.

Ade Jase. Jase. Jason

Jason lets Harry go. Harry retches catching his breath.

Jason That's for being a little cunt

Jason drinks from the bucket. Passes Ade the bucket.
Moves to Harry, offers Harry his hand. Pulls him up.

You okay, Harry? You alright?

Harry Yeah, grand

Jason slings his arm over Harry's shoulder. He puts
him in a headlock.

Jason He's my new pet. He's alright, in'he? This one? Eh?

Gives him a friendly slap on the cheek, lets him go.

Do this all the time, don't we, Ade?

Harry Just catching my breath

Jason You're doing well, mate, you're doing spot on.
What I like about you Harry is you don't complain

Harry Cheers

Jason This boy's a legend. An absolute legend. I'm going
to adopt him as my mascot. He's going to bring me luck

Harry Bloody hell, you boys play hard. Reminds me of
my mate, had his stag do out in Krakov, right, got cheap
flights. The whole package. Whitewater rafting in the
morning, Auschwitz in the afternoon, back to the hotel
for a shower, quick bite to eat then on to a sex club. I was
last man standing. Auschwitz, though, have you been?
You see the train tracks. Fuck me. What people do

Anyhow, we'd hired the back room of this bar and the
best man he got this prossie – bit skinny but nice face.

Sits the groom down on a chair and does this full-on strip show, down to her knickers, whipped cream on her tits and that. And then, I'm not lying, she unzips him, sprays some of the cream on his cock and starts noshing him off like she's not had a hot dinner in weeks. His dad's there, his uncle, father of the bride . . . And we're all like, 'We hope that's low fat! Cholesterol!' Shouting things. This is the best bit. Just as the groom's about to pop – and you can tell he's nearing blast off 'cause his eye's going like he's having an epi – this prossie shoves her hand down her pants, reaches back and flops out the biggest cock you have ever seen. Fucking ladyboy. We were like, 'Where the fuck's she been stashing that', 'cause she had this tiny thong on. It were like that magician who makes the Statue of Liberty disappear. And the groom's face? Fucking glorious. He cried a bit actually. Went a bit dark

Ade Am I losing my mind?

Jason Ignore him, Harry, he's got a short attention span. Whose go's it, I forgot?

Harry Definitely my turn

Jason Go on then, forfeit or dare?

Harry Hahahahahaha!

Jason What? What? You got one? Is it a good one?

Harry It's a bit mad

I dare you two to kiss each other. With tongues

Jason Alright

Don't do anything you're not comfortable with, Ade

Jason moves towards Ade. They are very close, noses almost touching.

Look at you. All serious

I got a better idea

Harry Go on, what is it?

Jason Why don't you kiss Ade?

Harry It's not my dare

Jason Don't matter. Think he likes you

Harry Does he?

Jason Yeah. Go on

Harry Fucking hell, never kissed a fella before

You sure he wants me to? He's got a right face on

Jason I don't think Ade knows what he wants, Harry

Or maybe he does. Maybe he just prefers to watch? It's a bit scary actually doing something, innit?

That it, Ade? I bet you watched me a lot. Kept up with all the games. Sky-Plussed it all. Bet you loved that tape. Did you though? Did you love it?

Go on. All you got to to do is reach out and take it. It's what I do. See how it tastes

Ade That what you want?

Ade moves to Harry. Kisses him. Ade shoves Harry off.

Harry Fuck's sake, mate, it's just a bit of lads' fun

Ade That what you want is it? That's what you're after?

Harry We was having a laugh

Ade Get out. Get the fuck out now. Now!

Harry Get your hands off me. Don't you touch me. Don't you fucking touch me

Ade Want me to call your manager?

Harry And tell him what, you're taking pills and trashed the room? Mouthy twat. I'll go when he says

Jason He's right, fuck off

You heard, off you trot, son

Harry Who'd you think you are? Acting all la-di-da 'cause you're famous?

Jason Go on, you was fun for a bit, I'm bored now

Harry You want to know something?

Jason Not really

Harry You're a shit footballer. Hey. When was the last time you saw your kids?

Jason grabs Harry, forces his face down into the bucket of vodka. Violently. They struggle a while.

Jason That's it. Good boy, good boy, good doggie

Ade drags Jason away from Harry. Harry coughs, splutters and retches, out of breath.

Harry Think we don't know what goes on? Kind of people he has in here? Lads up and down the stairs, all hours. Think we don't know?

Jason Be another story, Harry. One for your collection

Harry This is going on Twitter, mate

Jason Harry, son. I got people for that sort of thing. This goes on Twitter, I'll own your house. And your nan's house. And your children's house if you get that far in life. Just so you know. Now off you trot. Grown-ups talking

Harry exits.

D'you reckon he was showing off?

Oh what, you going all moody on me now?

Come on, Ade, we was having a laugh

That was pretty tame actually.

Ade What are you trying to prove?

Jason Prove? I'm not sure what

Ade Your life is so much better than mine 'cause you pull shit like this, is that it?

Jason Well, obviously you're fulfilled inside and yes, being insanely rich and famous is without meaning, but all things considered, it is a laugh

SIX

Jason and Ade in the same places.

Jason Look at your face! I wish you could see your face, it's so funny right now

What? What?

Ade What just happened?

Jason When?

Ade Just then

Jason I don't know what you're talking about

Ade All like, what? What, Ade? Like nothing just happened

Jason I honestly don't know what you're talking about. Truthfully

Ade I don't think you're well

Jason I'm tip-top. This is usual. What?

What is it you're after, I'm trying to keep it light here?

Ade Is a little sincerity too much to ask?

Jason Oh lovely, very few social occasions aren't enlivened by sincerity

Ade Now it's serious, now it's banter, now it's something else, always on your terms

Jason Sorry, can I have a second, just to get my listening face ready?

Ade This is what I mean. Twelve years, Jason, nothing. Then I get a text. Twelve years, you send a text

Jason What you want, a telegram?

Ade Some bullshit story about a quote for your villa, I think fine, that's how he wants to play it. So I come here and I ask again and you say, 'I just wanted to know if you'd come,' alright. But we both know that ain't no answer. It's a clever answer. Don't make it true

See, there are questions you ask when you're younger that as you get older they fade. But they never go away, not really. You turn up the noise around them so you can't hear them no more, but they're there. In the background. And sometimes, you get to a place in your life where the other voices go quiet, and you hear those old voices again

I'm asking you straight. And I don't want no bullshit about a villa. For once, take this serious. Or I'm leaving and I ain't coming back

One last time, why you ask me here?

Jason Truth?

I wanted you to fix up my villa

You wanted a view. A view

It's yours, Ade. The villa. I want you to have it. You could live there. I could visit. We could look at the view

My knee's chalk. I got X-rays. Ever seen a mountain crumble and fall into the sea? It could go any time. Years, months, days

You're the last thing I remember of any value

Ade You want us to move in to a villa together. In Greece

Jason I don't know why you're making a thing of it

Ade When I got your text, I admit, it touched my pride. You know, I thought those same voices I heard, he heard them too. I don't know, maybe I had some notion . . . But now I'm here, you know what I feel?

Jason Let me guess, Ade. Is it pity?

Ade Always got the clever answer. But that's all you got

Jason All I got? I scored goals that make grown men and women weep. I stopped people's hearts. Made time stand still. What you do?

Ade I found someone. And he loves me. And I love him. It ain't perfect but that's what it is

Jason That's lovely, Ade. It's a lovely sentiment. A loser's sentiment, but a nice one all the same

You was never cut out for what I was cut out for, that's the sum of it. I inspire love. Devotion. People despise me, I get people wishing me dead. What do you get, Ade, invoices?

Ade Least I live in the real world

Jason I live in the same world you do, just better parts of it

I flown on private jets. I been to parties on boats you can only dream of and fucked models so beautiful they turn you to stone

Trying to claim that somehow in this situation you have the moral high ground because you fix people's toilets for a living. 'Cause somehow failure is real? You haven't the nerve to live like I do. It would scare the shit out you

Want to know what it's like playing against the best? The speed of thought is incredible. They see things you don't, they see the world different. You're flat and they're in three dimensions. They're painting the Sistine Chapel and you're scratching a fucking boar on the wall of a cave. They're playing an entirely different game

I wasn't even close, mate. You was lucky. You found that out before you got going, it took me another ten years

Some people they love it. I had moments. But they was fleeting. Mostly I was terrified

You know why I never answered your calls? I didn't want to be infected by your failure. 'Cause it stains. It clings. And once it's on, you can't get rid of it

Ade Did you do it to get in my head?

Jason There's this room. They use it to see if astronauts can cope with space. It's in the States, I had some free time on a pre-season tour and I went. It's completely silent. They give you a chair 'cause you can't hear your own footfall and it does your balance. There's no such thing as silence. Your own heartbeat. Your own hair growing, your skin – your scalp makes a noise as it shifts. Like bugs crawling across your brain. This white noise. It's deafening

Ade I just want a straight answer, did you do it to get in my head?

Jason That's what I'm telling you. I don't know

SEVEN

Ade has gone. Jason stands in exactly the same place as he was at the end of the previous scene.
    He looks at the film playing on the television.
    He attempts to wrench the television from the wall. Fails.
    He makes a call from his mobile phone.

Jason The kids up?

I don't know, it's light

No wait

> *Cut off. Jason stares at the phone.*
> *He turns the shower on. Returns.*
> *He takes the vodka, moves to the balcony. Forces himself to drink the rest of the vodka. Looks out. Pulls a veil around his face.*
> *His mobile phone rings. He answers.*

Yeah

Sorry, what? Do I want an upgrade?

> *He doesn't end the call. Just lays the phone down.*
> *He clutches his head.*
> *He performs a few dummies and feints, muttering under his breath – his script.*
> *He turns the television up loud.*
> *He walks into the shower and scrubs himself.*
> *The noise in his head is deafening.*